HOCKEY PENGUIN

By Luke Anderson
With Contributions by Megan Anderson

To Ty,

Thanks for reading the Hockey Penguin series. I hope you love it. Happy Reading!

Chapter 1: Big News For The Chill

Tick tock. Tick tock. The clock counts down. A minute and two seconds. A minute one. One minute. The time on the scoreboard changes from minutes to seconds.

The Chill fight to get the puck out of their defensive zone, but the Jazz don't make it easy. Rodman T. Penguin, one of twelve South African penguins on the Chill, pokes the puck away from the captain of the all moose Jazz and races around the burly animal to snag the puck.

Play moves towards the other end of the ice where Rodman shoots a pass to his teammate, Jason Vyand. Two Jazz players race at Jason as he approaches the offensive zone. He's crowded. There's no way he can make it over the blue line onside. To his right, Pencil Spoedige clacks his stick on the ice, letting Jason know he's open. Instead of passing the puck, Jason slams on his breaks and holds it, causing Spoedige and two other Chill, Ty Mosienko and Pablo Pikkewyn, to cross the line offside. However, Jason's plan works. The approaching Jazz players slam into each other and fall to the ice.

The players offside hustle to get back behind the blue line, giving the Jazz enough time to regroup and set up on defense. Rodman carves up the ice on his way into the play. He blows past the other players in time to cross the blue line just behind Jason. He sets up to the side of the net. None of the Jazz players check him down. He whistles to Jason and motions with his head at a vulnerable spot of the net.

Jason looks at Rodman but doesn't pass the puck. Instead, he takes it behind the net to try a wrap around.

Rodman does his best to block the Jazz players out of Jason's way, and the other Chill get into position to collect a rebound if Jason misses.

Fifty-two seconds left.

Jason completes his wrap around with the help of Rodman, but the goalie moves to that side of the net and prevents Jason from scoring. In doing so, the goalie leaves the whole other side of the net wide open. Instead of shooting where he's blocked, Jason brings the puck in close to himself and holds it. He glides just past the reach of the goalie, who misses the puck with his glove. Jason aims and fires around the goaltender at the wide open net, but the puck bounces off the pole with a clang and back onto the ice. The Jazz scoop up the puck and head back on offense.

Jason stares at the net in disbelief.

Forty-six seconds left.

Rodman and the rest of the Chill hightail it back to the play. Pikkewyn checks the Jazz player with the puck against the glass hard, and the puck floats out into the open ice. Rodman collects it and weaves in and out, past and through defenders on his way back to the offensive zone.

Thirty-nine seconds left.

Rodman finds Spoedige in front of the net and shoots him a pass. Spoedige one times the puck at the goalie, but it's blocked by a mass of Jazz sticks that crowd the area. The puck gets passed out to Mosienko near the blue line. He rears back and fires. The shot goes over the goalie's head and behind the net.

Thirty-one seconds left.

Rodman and Jason race for the puck from opposite directions, both have Jazz players on their heels. Rodman wins the race to the puck, but Jason bumps him, causing both penguins to miss and leave the puck behind.

The puck ends up on the stick of one of the Jazz players, and play moves back the other way. Before the Jazz can get it out of the zone, like lightning, Spoedige sneaks up on the moose and steals the puck. With a clearing in front of the net, Spoedige fires. His shot is blocked and held by the Jazz goalie until whistles blow and play stops with twenty-three seconds left.

The Chill's coach, known only as The Coach, calls a timeout. Both teams head to their bench for last minute instructions. The Coach and his team huddle near the boards. "Ok guys listen up. We need one more goal to set records for points scored in a game, most lopsided win, and biggest shutout ever in Chill history. If we're to achieve this, it's going to take teamwork. Spoedige, Mosienko, you guys took some good shots out there. Jason, you might have had an assist opportunity if you'd have shot Rodman a one timer instead of trying that wrap around. Just keep an eye open out there. Look for the open man. Look for the open shot."

Behind them, whistles blow as the timeout ends. Both teams head near the Chill's offensive zone for a faceoff. Rodman lines up with Jason and Spoedige on his wing and Pikkewyn and Mosienko behind him. The puck drops, and Rodman hits it back to Pikkewyn. The Chill pass the puck for what seems like forever but still can't get an open shot.

Tick tock. Tick tock. Thirteen seconds left.

The crowd grows restless. They scream for the Chill to shoot the puck.

Mosienko takes the puck from one side of the blue line to the other as the Chill rotate positions, sending Rodman to the wing and Jason in front of the net.

Seven seconds left.

Mosienko shoots the puck across the blue line to Spoedige. He rears back and fakes a shot. The fake out draws some attention his way. He sees Rodman with a wide open shot at the net and fires him the puck.

Four seconds left.

Rodman launches a one time blast so hard at the net that it rumbles the whole arena. All heads, on and off the ice, turn and watch the puck sail across the icy floor. It's going to be a goal for sure. Rodman smiles in anticipation of making team history.

Then, just as the puck is about to go past the goalie, Jason's stick comes down and stops it. He grabs the puck, spins, and fires it right into the goalies leg pads.

The puck is stopped and time expires.

The final score is Chill 9, Jazz 0.

Rodman looks to his teammate dolefully. He wonders why Jason stopped the puck. The other Chill look at Jason with contempt.

Jason grits his beak and skates past them to the bench.

Though it isn't a record setting game, it is another shellacking of an opponent by the Capetown Chill, the greatest team ever to play hockey in South Africa history.

*

At practice the next day, the Chill carry out a drill in which Rodman, Spoedige, Pikkewyn and Andy Dapper act as the penalty kill team. Jason, Mosienko, P.V. Dermeer, Kurdt Fraiser, and Rugby Storm act as the power play unit. The power play is when a team has five players on the ice trying to capitalize on their odd man advantage against the penalty kill team,which has only four players and sometimes only three because a player or players have gone into the penalty box.

Rodman and the penalty kill crew wear white jerseys, and Jason and the power play unit wear green. Both sets of jerseys also have blue, red, yellow, and black strategically placed to make them look like the South African flag.

The penalty kill players form a diamond shape in front of the goalie. Each penguin defends a specific portion of the ice, sometimes defending two opponents at once. Rodman is paired up with Jason. He moves his stick exaggeratedly in front of Jason's stick, disrupting any timely shot or pass he might try to get off.

"You'll never get this puck away from me Rodman." Jason stands pat with the puck.

Others on the power play get into great scoring position and clack the ice with their sticks, sending echoes throughout the empty arena. Jason refuses to pass the puck. The clacks, light at first, grow louder and harder as his teammates practically beg for the puck.

"Watch me!" Rodman pokes the puck away.

The two penguins race for it. Rodman wins. He skates fast away from Jason towards the empty net at the other end of the rink. Jason pokes and taps at Rodman with his stick, but it does nothing to impede Rodman's breakaway. As Rodman approaches the empty net, Jason wraps the curved end of the stick around Rodman's waist and pulls back hard. Rodman spins, stumbles, and falls to his belly. Both puck and penguin slide into the net, setting off the goal light.

The Coach blows his whistle and makes a hooking penalty signal with his flippers. "Jason! Do that in a game and you'll needlessly put us on the penalty kill."

Jason grumbles indiscernibly and skates back to join the team, leaving Rodman crumpled up inside the net. With a smile on his face, Rodman pushes himself on his belly out of the net. He glides along the ice, stands up, and skates to rejoin his team. He squeezes into the huddle of players around The Coach.

The Coach holds a clipboard in his flippers. "Good practice today team. I have some big news. I don't want to get anyone's hopes up, but there's going to be a scout in the crowd tomorrow."

There's an excited uproar amongst the Chill.

"Where's the scout from?" Spoedige shouts.

"He's an Alaska Gold Rush scout from the International American Hockey League." The Coach has to quiet his team once more. "Ok. Ok. Ok. Calm down. I don't want anyone getting overly excited about this. He's coming with the team's general manager. They have an open spot on the team, and they're bringing *one* contract with them. Do me a favor guys. Don't try to be superstars tomorrow. Go out there and play Chill style hockey. That's why we have scouts coming to look at us in the first place."

The penguins skate off the ice with high hopes and big league dreams on their minds.

"Good practice Pikkewyn. Nice skating Spoedige." The Coach puts his flippers up and stops Rodman and Jason. "I need to talk to you two. Good practice Dolvy." Once the other players are off the ice, The Coach turns to Rodman and Jason. "Ok guys. I figure that the contract is going to end up in the flippers of one of you. You're my top guys. But, do me a favor. I need you to keep the others under control. Make sure no one gets too flashy or shows off out there tomorrow."

"Will do Coach!" Rodman beats Jason to the guarantee.

The Coach pats Rodman on the shoulder. "I knew I could count on you Rodman."

Jason looks at the interaction between Rodman and The Coach with disdain and jealousy. He decides at that moment to win the contract no matter what it takes.

"Well, I better get going. I have some game planning to do before tomorrow night's game." The Coach leaves Jason and Rodman alone.

"Wow! It's always been my dream to play for the Gold Rush," Rodman says.

"Well maybe next year." Jason moves in close to Rodman and takes a menacing stance.

"Next year?"

"Yeah. Next year. You don't really think the Gold Rush are going to take you over me do you?"

Rodman jumps into a faceoff position and smiles his big silly penguin smile. "They'd be fools not to take Ol' Hott Rod!"

Jason remains unmoved, not buying into Rodman's playful mood. "Oh brother! Are you kidding me? You really think that you're the best player on this team? The truth is, I'd be the captain if I had been here a year earlier than you."

Rodman stands back up. His smile dissipates. "Well Jason, we'll just have to see."

"Yeah! We will." Jason takes a step back and unexpectedly jumps into the faceoff position.

Quick on his toes, Rodman jumps into the faceoff position across from Jason.

"And I'm warning you Rodman, don't get in my way tomorrow." Jason uses his stick to bat Rodman's stick from his grasp and across the ice.

Rodman looks stunned. He doesn't like the tone in Jason's warning. With a furrowed brow, he stares a hole through the back of the agitated penguin's head as Jason skates to the tunnel. When he's out of sight, Rodman relaxes and fetches his stick.

*

After practice, Rodman, Chad "Dolvy" Doelverdediger, Spoedige, and Pikkewyn, walk along a tropical beach to their favorite hot spot. During the day, the waters on the beach are dazzlingly blue from afar and so sparklingly clear up close, the ocean floor is visible when standing in them.

Rodman and the others wear Hawaiian print shirts, sunglasses, and palm tree print swimming trunks. They pass by a variety of animals native to South Africa. Rhinos, giraffes, elephants, zebras, tortoises, and other penguins play beach volleyball, lift weights, cliff dive, build sand castles, and swim in the bay. The Chill are too lost in their thoughts of fame, fortune, and hockey stardom to notice the other animals around them.

"Oh boy! Can you believe the Gold Rush sent a scout all the way down here to see us?" Pikkewyn interrupts the others' thoughts.

"One of us could even make the team!" Spoedige throws his flippers in the air.

"It won't be me." Dolvy kicks a pebble out into the white sands of the beach.

"Why not you Dolvy?" Pikkewyn asks.

"They don't need a goalie. They have Jack Haas. You know. The quick as lightning rabbit."

"I think he's a hare," Spoedige corrects.

Pikkewyn turns his head to Rodman at the back of the line. "We all know who they're going to take anyway."

They all stop and look at Rodman.

Rodman, lost in thought, keeps walking and bumps into Dolvy. He looks around at his friends. "What?"

"I said, we all know who they're going to take," Pikkewyn repeats.

"Who?"

"The Gold Rush. They're going to pick you Rodman."

"You're the best player on the team," Spoedige agrees.

Rodman starts walking again. The others follow him to a tiki hut with a flashing sign that reads Klapper Kamer. "Come on guys. We all have a chance. Any one of us could have a stellar game out there tomorrow, or show something to those scouts that they like, and *boom!*" Rodman claps his flippers. "Contract."

"None of you guys have a chance at that contract tomorrow." Another group of penguins, led by Jason, walk out of the Klapper Kamer.

"What!?" Rodman is taken aback.

Jason points to himself as he speaks. "I'm getting that contract tomorrow, and there's nothing anyone can do to stop me."

"No way Jason. Rodman's twice as good as you are," Pikkewyn says.

"In your dreams. Just wait until tomorrow. I'm going to cream the competition. And, I'm going to win that contract." Jason motions for his cronies from the team to follow him.

They walk away, and Rodman's group walks into the restaurant. Inside, the Klapper Kamer is a raucous and happening place. Animals everywhere eat, drink juice, play cards, shoot darts, dance, and have an all out good time. The ceiling is made of straw and grass. The walls, floor, and juice bar are made of bamboo, and everything is tied together with rope. Banners for sports teams, movie posters, pictures of the Klapper Kamer's patrons, boat oars, ship steering wheels, life-rafts, signs, and a variety of other fun things litter the walls.

Rodman and his friends take a seat at one of the tables and order four passion fruit juices that come in coconut cups with tiny umbrellas.

"Boy oh boy! I can't believe the gall of that Jason." Dolvy leans back in his chair.

"Yeah! He really thinks he's something," Spoedige concurs.

"Don't worry about him guys. We just have to go out there tomorrow and play our game," Rodman says.

"I wouldn't put it past Jason to try something to make the rest of us look bad out there tomorrow," Spoedige says.

"We'll just have to watch each other's backs, but, let's not think about him right now." Rodman raises his cup. "Let's make a toast. To the Chill."

The other penguins raise their glasses. A toast is made and cheers go around the table. The penguins tap their cups together and drink their passion fruit juice.

Chapter 2: The Contract Game

The wait for the next game has everyone anxious. The locker room is abuzz with laughter, energy, and anticipation as the Chill put on their gear and prep their equipment. They tape their sticks, sharpen their skates, and polish their helmets. Everyone is excited. Everyone, that is, except Jason. His skates are already sharpened, his uniform on, and his stick taped. He leans back in his chair glaring at Rodman.

Rodman pays no attention to Jason. He laces up his skates, lost in thought about winning the Gold Rush contract. Since the age of three, when he first started playing hockey, he's taken seven peewee hockey teams, all four high school teams, all four college teams, and three times the Chill to the finals. He didn't win them all, but he has fourteen championships to show for all his hard work. Now, with tonight's game, he has the chance to become a professional player and play for the ultimate hockey championship, the Anderson Cup.

"Tonight's the night," Rodman whispers to himself. He reaches for a red and white striped scarf in his locker. "Nothing can stop me as long as I have my lucky scarf and my trusty stick."

Since high school, Rodman hasn't played a game without his stick or the scarf that was awarded to him by Alaska Gold Rush great and former Chill, Sol Kampion, after his first peewee championship.

Rodman begins to put his scarf on but stops when he's called by The Coach.

"Yeah Coach?"

"I need to see you in my office." The Coach motions for Rodman to come.

Rodman sets his scarf down. With a charismatic waddle amplified by walking across the floor in his skates, he scampers off to The Coach's office.

Jason looks at Rodman's locker and then at the other players in the locker room. They're all too caught up with excitement to notice him, so Jason reaches into his bag and pulls out a green box labeled Sleepytime Tea. He takes the tea to Rodman's locker and mixes it with his passion fruit juice. Not satisfied with the potential potency of one packet of Sleepytime Tea, Jason mixes in four more packages.

After the mixture of tea and juice, Jason moves onto Rodman's stick. He gives the locker room another look to make sure no one's watching. The coast is clear, so he sets the stick on the ground and gives it swift stomp, completely cracking the blade from the handle. To mask the broken blade, Jason uses Rodman's hockey tape to tape the broken pieces together, giving the stick the appearance of being just fine. On the ice though, the stick will be as useful to Rodman as a dead fish.

Jason's head whips around at the sound of the handle of The Coach's office door turning. Rodman starts to step out but stops to tell The Coach one last thing. Jason uses the time he has left to stuff Rodman's lucky scarf into a pocket in his hockey pants and waddle quickly back to his own locker. He plops down in his seat and pretends to lace up his skates just as Rodman emerges from the office, oblivious to all of Jason's misdoings.

Rodman walks through the locker room with a lot of pep in his step and his trademark smile on his beak. He shoots Jason a thumbs up as he passes his teammate by.

Back at his locker, Rodman reaches for his passion fruit juice and takes a big gulp. His face contorts. The taste is quite different and a little unpleasant. He looks suspiciously into the glass. A single tiny fragment of a tea leaf floats around the top. He digs it out, examines it, and flicks the leaf away. Though a bit puzzled by the odd taste of the drink, he guzzles it down anyway. He reaches for his scarf after his drink is finished, but it's not where he left it. He scratches his head perplexed. He looks for it all throughout the locker room, under his table, under other players' chairs and tables, and inside the extra stick container, crawling halfway in, poking around the bottom of the giant bucket with his tail sticking out of the top. Near the buffet table, Dolvy tries to take a bite from a fish sandwich, but Rodman stops him so he can check for his scarf inside the sandwich first. He even resorts to dumping out the locker room garbage can and rummaging through the trash. Unable to find it, he slumps down amongst the garbage.

"Where can it be?" Rodman frowns and puts the trash back into the can. Then, he looks towards The Coach's office. Perhaps he left it in there. He waddles back to the office and lets himself in without knocking.

The Coach looks up at the intrusion and watches Rodman poke around his office.

Rodman looks under the chair he was sitting in, all the way around The Coach's desk, on The Coach's desk, and in a wastebasket by the wall. The scarf is nowhere to be found. Rodman makes his way to a locker along the far wall and rummages through it.

Finally, The Coach has had enough. "Can I help you Rodman?"

"Lost my lucky scarf Coach. I might have left it in here a minute ago," Rodman answers.

"Rodman! You didn't go in my locker." The Coach stands up.

Rodman comes out of the locker panicked. "I know Coach. But, I have to find it."

"Maybe you left it in your locker. Did you check there?"

"I'm pretty sure I took it out, but I'll go check." Rodman leaves his coach's office again.

Back in the locker room, Rodman's smile is no longer upon his face. He passes by Jason, who sees the misery all over Rodman's face and shoots Rodman a sarcastic thumbs up.

Rodman throws a variety of items out of his locker. Books, old candy bar wrappers, pucks, gloves, a half eaten fish sandwich, and other random items fly out of the locker until it is completely empty. He even checks every hanger inside his locker, but he finds only his other uniforms.

Out of the corner of his eye, pretending to check on his own stick, Jason takes in all of Rodman's trepidation and revels in it.

Rodman slumps down into his chair deflated. "Oh no."

The Coach comes out of his office and shouts, "Game time everyone. Let's go!"

The Chill jump to their feet. The butterflies in their tummies flutter as the excitement reaches an all time high. They all race out of the locker room, except Rodman, who gets up slowly. He panics for a moment at the realization that he hasn't had a chance to tape up his stick. He grabs it, perplexed too see it's already taped. He dismisses his concerns and convinces himself that he must have taped it up and doesn't remember. Usually the first one sprinting out of the locker room, leading his team to the ice, Rodman jogs out pulling up the rear.

*

Rodman and the Chill run their skates over the ice as they stand near the blue line. Across from them, on the other blue line, stand their opponents for a second straight night, the South African Jazz, in their white uniforms with blue trim. Their logo, a blue music note coming from a trumpet, sits across their chests. Throughout the national anthem, Rodman yawns as the Sleepytime Tea kicks in.

The anthem ends, and both teams take their faceoff positions. Rodman and the center for the Jazz, Eland Kop, drop their sticks. Eland grunts at Rodman so heavily the flaps of his lips vibrate. Rodman smiles at him not intimidated.

The referee drops the puck. Rodman fights for it, but his weakened stick bends, and the puck is taken by Eland. Rodman feels the difference in his stick and checks it out. The momentary distraction allows Eland to bowl him over. The hit takes him by surprise, but Rodman quickly picks himself off the ice and rushes to get back into the game.

One of the Jazz players takes a shot at Dolvy. The Chill goalie blocks the shot, but it bounces off his chest padding and out to Eland, who rears back and blasts another shot. This time, Jason uses his body to block the puck, preventing it from even reaching Dolvy.

In the stands, the Alaska scout, a pig named Copper Cashbrenner, and their general manager, a snake named Coil Wraparound, take notice of the goings on in the game. Coil whispers to Copper, and the pig jots some notes in a book. Behind them sits a monkey wearing a safari hat. He leans forward and tries to peek into their notebook, but he can't see anything.

Spoedige collects the puck and pass it out of his defensive zone to Rodman. Two nearby Jazz defenders try to cut off the pass, but they end up running into each other. Rodman grabs the puck with his damaged stick, and thought it bends a little, he's able to maintain control. With the defenders on the ice, Rodman skates away on a breakaway. The other players give chase, but Rodman has a huge lead.

Jason looks on mortified. He wants nothing less than for Rodman to score any goal in the game, much less the first goal.

Rodman approaches the net with a quickness. The Jazz goalie skates out a bit in anticipation of Rodman's shot, trying to cut off any angles that would make it easy for Rodman to shoot around him. Rodman knows he can sink the shot anyway. He rears back, aims his shot, and times it accurately. He swings his stick, knowing he's got an easy goal and a head start in the eyes of the Alaska scout. With a ferocious blast, he hits the puck, but all the force of the hit is taken away by the give of his broken stick. The puck glides softly to the goalie, who easily scoops it up with his glove hand.

Jason lets out a sigh of relief.

Rodman stops in front of the goalie and examines his stick again. He can tell underneath the tape the stick is cracked in two. Before he can turn around to get back in the game, Eland levels him again, this time from behind. Rodman hits the ice tummy and face first with a thud. He winces in pain as the play moves back towards Dolvy.

Jason skates to Rodman. "Get up Rodman. Get off the ice if your stick is broken. Don't hang around making the rest of us look bad."

In the stands, Copper makes more notes in his book. The monkey scoots closer and tries to peek at the notebook again. He can make out just a few words but not enough to know what is being noted. Copper, sensing he's being watched, turns his head slightly to confirm his suspicions. The monkey jumps back into his seat, pretending to watch the game.

Rodman skates gingerly back to the bench with a yawn. Fraiser jumps over the wall to take his spot. Rodman sits at the end of the bench near Baruti, the team's equipment manager.

"Can I get you a new stick Rodman?" Baruti asks.

"I guess I'm going to have to use a new one." Rodman holds up his broken stick for Baruti to see the dangly blade.

"Don't worry Hott Rod. I've got a fine stick for you." He waddles to the equipment rack, rummages through a few sticks, and pulls out a stick labeled Pro Power 5000 X. Satisfied with his pick, he brings the stick to Rodman. "Here you go."

Rodman holds it in his flippers and tries to get a feel for it. It's a good stick for sure, but it's not his stick.

Baruti notices the discomfort on Rodman's face. "It's the best team stick we've got."

"It'll do." Rodman fakes a smile and yawns animatedly.

"Rodman! You got a new stick?" screams The Coach from the other end of the bench.

"Yes sir Coach!" Rodman holds up his new stick.

"Good. Here comes Spoedige. Get back out there."

"Yes sir Coach!" Despite his lack of energy, Rodman jumps over the wall.

Jason follows Spoedige to the bench and bumps Rodman with his shoulder.

Rodman doesn't let Jason get to him. He knows the best thing he can do is play hard and help his team in any way he can.

Helping his team isn't easy though with the absence of his lucky scarf weighing on his mind, the uncomfortable stick in his flippers, and the Sleepytime Tea taking a toll on his awareness. Rodman loses faceoff after faceoff. He maneuvers listlessly around the ice, finding it hard to catch up to and stay with the Jazz. He even botches a pass that allows the Jazz to get a breakaway that leads to a goal. Rodman gets checked hard against the glass, gets knocked down over and over, has the puck poked away, and when Pikkewyn slaps a one-timer his way, he misses it and the puck is collected by the Jazz. For Rodman, each shift feels like an entire game's worth of hockey.

Each time Rodman makes a mistake or does something detrimental for his team, Copper notes it in his book with a frown or a disapproving shake of his head. Likewise, each time Jason does something positive, Copper makes another note with a nod and a smile. Each time he makes a new note, the monkey tries to sneak a peek at what it says.

Coil notices the monkey peeking at them now too and turns to him. "Can I help you with something?"

"Oh!" says the monkey with a start. "No thank you."

They remain locked in a long silent stare before Coil finally turns back to finish the game. The monkey spits his tongue out at them. Coil, with a keen sense of hearing, turns quickly around just as the monkey pulls his tongue back into his mouth.

Jason plays an excellent game. He scores a goal on a one timer from Mosienko. He blocks several shots from reaching Dolvy. His passing is impeccable, never losing the puck on a takeaway. His moves are crisp. He's so good that he draws defenders towards him several times, leaving his teammates wide open to take good shots. Twice they score on those passes. At times, he seems to be a one man show. He even picks off passes meant for other players on his team, takes shots in traffic when he should pass the puck, and uses his own players as decoys for checks meant for him.

Rodman finishes the game on the bench. He watches with contempt as Jason shows off during the final seconds. Sandwiched between Spoedige and Dapper, Rodman sits ashamed, humbled, and upset with his performance. His head slumped into his flippers and his eyes half shut, he wears a pitiable frown.

"Don't worry Rodman." Spoedige pats him on the back. "It just wasn't your night. Those guys from Alaska might not even care how you played tonight. There's a chance they've seen some old footage and made their choice a long time ago."

"Maybe," Rodman says halfheartedly.

The final buzzer goes off. The score is Chill 4, Jazz 3. Copper and Coil go over their notes. Desperate to see what they've written, the monkey creates a distraction by throwing a banana peel over the head of Copper, landing it on the pig's dress shoes.

"Ugh!" Copper cries. He sets the notebook down in perfect view for the monkey to read over his notes as he tends to his shoes. All the notes are about how great a player they believe Jason to be and how he is going to make an already great team a superpower in the IAHL. The notes on Rodman aren't so favorable, stating that he won't ever make it in the IAHL as he doesn't even seem be able to keep pace in the minor leagues.

The monkey is engrossed in the notes when he is scared nearly out of his safari hat by the vicious hissing of Coil in his face.

"Get out of there!" The snake's tongue flickers as he talks.

The monkey jumps up and runs as fast as he can out of the arena.

Jason's game stats include one goal, two assists, and zero penalties. Rodman finishes with zero goals, zero assists, and two tripping penalties from sleepily stumbling and taking out Jazz players.

The Chill, except Rodman, who walks behind them with The Coach, make a mad dash for the locker room. They're all eager to see who's won the contract. Spoedige had the game winning goal and feels he has a legitimate shot at it. Pikkewyn had a goal and an assist and also feels he has a shot.

The Coach throws a flipper around Rodman's shoulder sympathetically. "Tough game Rod. If you'd like, I can still put in a good word for you."

"That's ok Coach. I don't want to hurt anyone else's chances."

The Coach pats him on the back as they walk through the tunnel.

*

Sometime after the game, Rodman sits at his locker still in his uniform. The rest of the Chill have changed out of their uniforms and await the Alaska personnel. Disheartened and sleepy, Rodman knows he isn't the winner of the contract, yet he can't make himself leave before it's presented. He knows it's wrong, but he can't help hoping Jason doesn't get the contract. He doesn't appreciate the way Jason didn't listen to The Coach and displayed no leadership qualities tonight. He was clearly out for himself and the contract, not for the good of the team.

The locker room doors open. Copper walks and Coil slithers into the room. Both wear tailor made, light blue suits with white shirts and light blue, gold, and black striped neckties, the colors of the Gold Rush.

Rodman stares into his locker, unable to look them in the eye.

The Coach brings the Gold Rush personnel to the center of the room and asks for everyone's attention. All eyes lock onto the pig and the snake.

"Hello everyone. My name is Copper Cashbrenner. I'm the head scout for the Alaska Gold Rush. It was a pleasure to watch you play. I know that most of you were expecting me tonight, but I don't know if you were expecting the man to my left. Allow me to introduce our general manager and head coach, Coil Wraparound."

Coil slithers in front of Copper. "Hello everyone. You have a fine team. I look forward to meeting each and every one of you, but first we have a bit of business to conduct."

There's a cheer amongst the Chill. Copper and Coil retreat with The Coach to his office. Before they shut the door, Coil whispers into The Coach's ear.

The Coach turns to his teams.

This is the moment they've all been waiting for. The Coach is going to call one of their names and change their life forever. They all hold their breath.

"Jason, could you come here for a minute?" The Coach calls.

Jason smiles arrogantly. He stands up and walks to The Coach's office with an annoyingly superior swagger. The excitement that had filled the room just seconds ago is gone. The other players go back to their postgame activities.

Rodman pulls off his jersey and chucks it into his locker.

Chapter 3: Second Chance

Upon seeing Jason called into The Coach's office, it was Rodman's plan to leave the building. Instead, he finds himself showering, cleaning up his locker, watching game footage, examining his broken stick, and giving the locker room another look for his scarf. By the time he gives up the search, everyone but The Coach has left, and the lights have been turned off.

Rodman sits in a chair in almost total darkness outside his locker and reflects on the night. The only light in locker room comes from the window of The Coach's office. That light too goes out too.

The Coach exits his office and catches a glance of Rodman sitting in the dark. He turns on the light in the locker room. "Rodman? You still here?"

"Yeah. I'm still here."

"What are you doing my boy?" The Coach makes his way to Rodman.

"Nothing. I just don't feel like leaving yet."

"Don't let this get you down kid. You're still an exceptional player. The best I've ever seen. If you ask me, the Gold Rush made a mistake. And their mistake, I feel, is our fortune. We're mighty glad to have you Hott Rod."

"Thanks Coach." Rodman fights back a tear. Inside his head he's devastated knowing he let a chance at his dreams slip away, but he's also at peace knowing he's thought of so highly by the Chill.

"I have to split kid. Don't stay too late eh?" The Coach walks to the door and stops. "One more thing Rod. This isn't the end for you. You'll have plenty of chances."

The Coach leaves.

Rodman is alone again, but he doesn't stay long. He feels a little better after hearing The Coach talk about other chances. He gets up and heads outside the arena. He's met by Jason and his cronies. They're huddled around looking at Jason's official IAHL contract. Rodman can hear them talking, and quickly The Coach's words no longer bring him solace.

He tries to slip past them unseen, but Jason spots him. "Hey Rodman. Come see my contract."

"No thanks Jason, but congratulations."

"Come on Rodman. Don't be a sore loser. Come take a look, and then we'll all go out and get a fish sandwich to celebrate."

Feeling the effects of the Sleepytime Tea more than ever, Rodman yawns exaggeratedly. "I can't Jason. I'm really tired."

"Suit yourself," says Jason.

The knot in Rodman's stomach tightens as he walks away hearing the laughter of the others.

*

Jason and his cronies celebrate that night at the Klapper Kamer. They sit around a table eating fish sandwiches and drinking passion fruit juice. They're obnoxious celebrating is so loud that it agitates the monkey in the safari hat seated behind them, trying to enjoy a banana split.

Jason slams his coconut cup on the table. Passion fruit juice flies all over the place. The noise made by the slam startles the monkey and several other patrons. "Oh boy. What a night. I have to tell you fellas, this is the greatest night of my life. I woke up this morning a big fish in a little pond. Now... now I'm a big fish in a big pond!" Jason laughs hysterically.

Jason whips his cup in the air over his head, sending more juice flying. It lands on the safari hat of the monkey behind him. The monkey gnashes his teeth and clenches his fist.

"I propose a toast!" Jason offers up his cup for everyone around. "To me!"

Despite their irritation with his egotism, Jason's cronies extend their cups to his.

Jason throws his drink back into his beak carelessly, spilling some of it from the sides of his mouth. The orange colored juice dribbles down his chin to his chest. He wipes it into his shirt with his flipper.

The other penguins have seen him act like this before, but never this over-the-top.

"Ok. Ok. Ok. So I have a confession to make." Jason stops to make sure he has their undivided attention. "It wasn't just my superb play tonight that won me the contract. Do you guys know why Rodman played so poorly?"

The other penguins look at each other and shrug.

Jason pulls Rodman's scarf out of his pocket and twirls it over his head. "Because I stole his lucky scarf!"

The monkey overhears this and shakes his head disapprovingly.

Jason's cronies are just as disapproving. They can't believe that even Jason would sabotage one of their own teammates.

"That doesn't mean anything. It's not like he played bad because he didn't have his scarf." Rugby waves his flipper at Jason, dismissing his words.

Jason leans into the table and holds a flipper over his mouth to prevent his words from carrying too far. "I also broke his stick and taped it up, making it look like it was ok when he was in The Coach's office."

The monkey can't believe what he's hearing.

"But he got another stick didn't he?" Kurdt asks.

Jason furrows his brow. "He got another one, but you guys know how crazy he is about his stick. It took all the wind out of his sails having to use that team stick, and do you know what else?"

"There's more?" P.V. asks.

Jason beams with pure evil. "Did you guys notice how tired he was? I poured five packets of Sleepytime Tea into his passion fruit juice before the game, and he drank the whole glass. He could barely keep his eyes open out there. He kept getting slammed all around the boards, and falling down, and tripping, and struggling to keep up with everyone."

Jason laughs like a madman, but his cronies don't join him.

The monkey bangs his fist against his table.

Jason stops laughing when he sees his cronies staring at him with contempt and not laughing. "What's the matter with you guys?"

"How do we know you didn't sabotage us too?" Mosienko rumbles.

"What?" Jason is shocked.

"Your cheap tricks could have hurt the whole team," Rugby backs up Mosienko.

"Well, if that's how you're going to be, I have bags to pack. You guys would have been smart to try something more to get the contract."

The monkey stands up and joins the penguins at their table. He gets in Jason's face and pokes him in the chest with his long fingers. "You're not smart. You're a jerk. And if I wasn't from another team, I'd tell the Gold Rush what you did."

Shockwaves are sent through Jason. He cautiously side steps the angry monkey and makes haste to the exit. A safe distance away, he turns and sees everyone scowling at him. He shoots them an arrogant smile before leaving. It doesn't matter to him if Rodman catches on with another IAHL team. The Gold Rush are the best team in the league, and he knows he'll only make them better.

The monkey pulls up Jason's vacated chair and sits with Rugby, Kurdt, Mosienko, and P.V. "Allow me to formally introduce myself. I'm Safari Chip, new owner, general manager, scout, and head coach of the Las Vegas Gamblers."

"The Gamblers!?" Kurdt asks.

"Yep," Safari Chip answers.

"Of the IAHL?" P.V. asks.

"Uh huh."

"The worst team in the league?" Rugby asks unaware of the question's negative implication.

"Uh, yeah," Safari Chip answers embarrassed. "But hopefully not for long. Could one of you tell me how I can get ahold of your coach so I can pull up some footage of Rodman?"

Rugby pulls a cell phone from his pocket and hands it to Safari Chip.

*

Inside the Chill video room, Safari Chip watches films of Rodman. The all-star penguin skates past, around, and over defenders. He scores goals, assists on goals scored by his teammates, and picks off passes. In some footage, Dolvy has fallen down or is out of position, and Rodman acts as the goalie, blocking up to three shots at one time using his stick and skates. He scores as he falls down, while deking or faking out defenders, from on or beyond the blue line, on wrap arounds behind the net, and on empty nets. He scores by shooting the puck off of opponent's skates, through heavy traffic, and by going five hole on the goalie, which means between the goalie's legs.

By the end of the tapes, Safari Chip sits with his jaw dropped. He can't believe the Gold Rush made their decision based on one game. With all their success, had they grown too arrogant in their decision making? Safari Chip doesn't care. He's just glad they slipped up.

The Coach turns the light on in the video room. "Now uhhh, Mr..."

"Chip. Safari Chip."

"Yes Mr. Chip. You say you were in the crowd tonight?"

"Yeah. I knew the Gold Rush were going to be scouting here, so I came too. I figured since they're so good and we're so bad I'd take a look at what they're looking at. Heaven knows we could use a high caliber player," Safari Chips explains.

"So you want to offer Rodman a contract?"

"Yeah. Do you think I have a shot at signing him?"

"I don't know. He's had his heart set on being a Gold Rush since he was a peewee." The Coach ponders the monkey's question a second longer. "But, Rodman's a smart guy. I think he'll realize this is a great opportunity. I still can't believe Jason would do this to him."

"I don't even want to talk about that guy." Safari shakes his head animatedly.

The two coaches talk, and the very late night turns into very early morning. They decide to surprise Rodman with the news before tomorrow night's game. They know Rodman could use a good surprise after what he's been through.

*

Less than twenty-four hours after having blown his shot at a Gold Rush contract, Rodman sits near his locker. His jersey and pads are on, his new stick is taped, and his skates are sharpened. He stares at a picture of himself as a youngster in peewee hockey being awarded a trophy and his lucky scarf by Sol Kampion.

The Coach comes out of his office and yells to his players, "Ok everyone. Game time!"

The Chill head for the locker room exit without nearly as much zest as they had a night ago. Rodman, still their captain, tries to lead his team out of the locker room.

"Not you Rodman." The Coach stops him.

"Why not Coach?" he asks.

"I think you might need the night off. I know you're taking it kind of hard that Jason got the contract, and I don't want to rush you back on the ice."

"No way Coach. I'm ready to go. I'm the captain. Those guys need me out there. I *want* to play Chill hockey!"

"Listen to me kid. Take the night off. It's not a request," orders The Coach.

Rodman's shoulders slump. He doesn't understand why he's not being allowed to play. The frustration is enough that he bangs his stick on the ground. The one thing that can cheer him up is playing hockey.

With the wink of an eye, The Coach lets Rodman off the hook. "There's something in my office that might help you clear your head."

Rodman raises an intrigued eyebrow. The Coach leaves, and Rodman cautiously approaches the office door. He pokes his head inside and sees Safari Chip in his safari hat, reading glasses, and a three piece suit sitting at The Coach's desk, scribbling in a notebook.

Upon seeing Rodman, Safari Chip sets down his pen and takes off his glasses. "Rodman T. Penguin! Come in. Come in." He walks over and grabs Rodman's flipper, forcibly shaking it. Safari Chip puts his arm around the puzzled penguin and directs him to the only other chair in the office. "Have a seat Rodman." Safari Chip sets Rodman down and makes his way back to The Coach's chair.

"Who are you?"

"Sir, my name is Safari Chip. I am the new owner, general manager, lead scout, and head coach of the Las Vegas Gamblers."

"The Gamblers!?" Rodman asks surprised.

"Yes sir."

"Of the IAHL?" Rodman asks still surprised.

"The one and only."

"The worst team in the league?" Rodman asks unaware of the question's negative implications.

"Ummm, yes," Safari Chip replies somewhat embarrassed for the second time in less than a day. "But, hopefully not for long! It's come to my attention that the Chill have a very special player. Someone who is ready to make a splash in the IAHL, so I sent myself down here to find that player."

"Oh. You mean Jason Vyand. The Gold Rush signed him last night."

Safari Chip stands up and slams his fist on the desk, scattering papers all over the place. He paces back and forth behind the desk. "No, not Jason Vyand! That no good two timing jerk. No Rodman. I came for you. I've seen the tapes on you and Jason, and let me tell you sonny boy," Safari Chip stops pacing and points at Rodman, "You take the cake. You have that poor guy totally school-boyed in all facets."

"I do?"

"Of course you do! Just because you had a bad game last night..."

"You saw that?" Rodman interrupts.

"Yeah."

"And you still want me on your team?"

Safari Chip places his hands on The Coach's desk for support and leans forward. He gets right into Rodman's face. "That's what I'm trying to say my man. You're the best player not only on the Chill, but in the entire country of South Africa. With your moves, you might even be better than anyone currently in the IAHL. I know it's a long shot that a team like us could ever sign a player with your talent, but we're willing to give you anything you want."

Rodman's eyes grow wide. He wears a huge smile. Big league dreams race through his head once more. Safari Chip slides him a Las Vegas Gamblers contract and a pen. Rodman doesn't read a word of the contract. He looks over the official IAHL stamp, the Gamblers logo, and the signatures of Safari Chip and the IAHL president. It's a thrill just holding it. Rodman suddenly remembers how The Coach told him he'd have plenty of other shots. What if one of those shots was with the Gold Rush? There's always next season. And what about the Chill? The Coach had just let him know how happy they were to still have him. This is going to be a tough decision. His smile fades, and he looks at Safari Chip. "I don't know. I might have to think about it for a day or two."

Safari Chip had hoped to avoid resorting to this, but he doesn't want to lose a chance at signing Rodman. "How long would you have to think about it if I told you that last night Jason Vyand stole your lucky scarf, cracked the blade off of your hockey stick and then taped it back up, and poured five packets of Sleepytime Tea into your passion fruit juice? All in an effort to make you look bad in front of the Alaska scout, and this is your chance to get into the IAHL and get some revenge."

"Did he really do that?"

"I heard him confess all of that after the game last night at the Klapper Kamer."

Rodman's eyes go wide with disbelief. He knew something was up with Jason the other night. He was playing like a one man team out there. They have never been the best of friends, but Rodman always thought they at least had a mutual respect for one another.

Safari Chip holds out the pen once more for Rodman.

"Give me that!" Rodman grabs the pen and signs the contract with a quickness.

Safari Chip couldn't beam any brighter if he were on fire. He gambled on this South African scouting trip, and by some luck he hit the jackpot, landing the best player the Gamblers have ever had, and quite possibly the best player to ever play the game. He's super excited to get back to Las Vegas and introduce Rodman to the team and the city. His thoughts are interrupted by Rodman.

"One question though."

Safari Chip looks at him in anticipation of the question.

"Just how bad are the Gamblers?"

Chapter 4: Rodman Arrives In Las Vegas

Rodman and Safari Chip sit in cozy leather chairs inside the Gamblers private plane. The stewardess serves Rodman a tall cold passion fruit juice. His travel with the Chill was mostly by bus.

"I've never flown first class before."

"Well, get used to it. When you play with the Gamblers, we make sure you have the best travel, the best living arrangements, the best food, the best medical staff, and the best everything really." Safari Chip counts each benefit on his fingers.

"Wow! If I get this sort of treatment on the last place team, I can only imagine how Jason's getting treated in Alaska."

*

Crammed like a sardine in a can, Jason rides inside a rundown tour bus. The bus is boisterous with chatter from its riders, and its obnoxious bouncing over an old broken road adds to Jason's agitation. Next to him, an overweight polar bear rests his sleeping head on Jason's shoulder. Jason tries to push the polar bear's head away, but the bear doesn't budge. Jason gives up until he feels a puddle of drool form on his shoulder. He gives the bear a violent shove, waking him up with a snarl. Jason points to the drool, but the polar bear is unapologetic.

Instead of traveling with Coil and Copper as they scout one last player, Jason opted to get to Alaska immediately by taking a commercial flight and then this bus. In his current predicament, he wishes he had gone with Copper and Coil in their luxury plane.

Still a hundred and forty mile away from the hotel, the bus maneuvers raucously through treacherous, curvy, windy, and icy mountains. A brutal bump causes the bus, and everyone in it, to bounce out of their seats. Jason hits his head on the roof and lands forcefully on his tail. He rubs his head with his flipper and hears a loud hiss coming from outside the motionless bus.

The driver exits the bus, checks something, and gets back on. "Flat tire folks. It's going to be a while."

Jason sighs. He has to fight his way through the crowded bus to get off and stretch his legs.

*

In the comfy confines of their first class style accommodations, Safari Chip finishes sending a text message to the Gamblers marketing department and then reaches into an opened briefcase. He pulls a picture from it and sets the picture of a bald turtle wearing a sheepish smile and a Gamblers jersey on a tray in front of them. "That's our goalie, Harlan T. Turtle."

Rodman examines the photo. "He looks like a good guy."

"Oh, he's a great guy. He just can't tend goal. Whenever our opponents shoot at him, he retreats into his shell."

Rodman wonders why anyone scared of the puck would ever put themselves into a position where a five pound frozen piece of rubber flies at them at a hundred miles an hour. "Does he ever stop it?"

"Sometimes, but it's purely accidental when he does." Safari Chip reaches into his briefcase and pulls out another photo. In it is a light grey mouse with enormous pink ears and black whiskers. "That's Liten Mus. He's from Germany, where he was an all-star."

"Was an all-star? What happened?"

"He played in an all mice league in Germany. When he came to America, he found out he'd be playing with cats, birds, and other predatory type animals. Now, he's more concerned with staying alive than playing hockey." Safari Chip sighs slightly and reaches back into his briefcase. "So, we went out and got Liten some help. Some muscle. Some protection if you will." Safari Chip lays two more photos on the tray. The first is a black and white Shih Tzu with messy fur about his face, big brown eyes slightly further apart than normal, and heavy whiskers that grow out like a handlebar mustache. The second is an all black Lhasa Apso, with slightly curly fur atop his head, dark eyes, and he's clean shaven except for a thin, extra long, white goatee. Both shabby and choppily trimmed dogs wear a devilish smile that lets Rodman know immediately that they're pranksters and trouble makers. "In order to provide Liten some protection, we went out and signed two of the toughest defensemen we could find. The black and white is Keith Kane and the all black is Morty Curtains. We call him Undertaker."

"Undertaker?" Rodman's eyebrows shoot up at the ominous name.

"Yep."

"Why Undertaker?"

"Because when he hits the opposition, they usually end up being carted off the ice on a stretcher. When we first got him, he injured so many players that other teams would have to forfeit due to lack of capable players."

"I'm guessing Undertaker and Kane didn't help Liten?"

"Well, they do but only for a short while. Because their hits are often violent and illegal, they end up in the penalty box. And, they like to hit the opposition… a lot," Safari Chip pounds a fist into his free palm, smashing and grinding it, representative of dogs' play.

"So, when they go to the box, Liten is playing scared again," Rodman notes.

"And furthermore, we're too often on a five on three penalty kill." Safari Chip digs around for another photo. He pulls out a picture of a suave smiling koala bear. He has a big, furry, grey head with white trim around his ears and eyes. Safari Chip hands Rodman the photo. "This is our right winger, Sammie Lou."

Rodman looks over the photo. "What's his story?"

"He comes to practice tired. He comes to games tired. He comes to autograph signings, photo shoots, and team meals tired. We've had him checked out by doctors and nothing's wrong. No one can figure out why he's always fatigued."

"Did anyone check his passion fruit juice for Sleepytime Tea?" Rodman plops back into his seat and folds his flippers.

Safari Chip chuckles uncomfortably. "Ummm no. The funny thing is he was an all-star in Fort Collins, Fresno, and Albuquerque in the AKHL. When he came to Las Vegas, he started out great, but now we can hardly get him to come to practice. And when he shows up, he's half asleep."

Rodman mulls the information. "Hmmm?"

"Those are the starters." Safari Chip holds out three more photos for Rodman to take. "And these are the backups."

Rodman looks at the photos of the other players: an albino grizzly cub, complete with the kind of teddy bear looks that make little girls oooh and ahhh, a brown miniature stallion with a shifty grin, pearly white teeth, a raised eyebrow, and a messily stylish mane, and a cream colored goose with feathers atop his head tied up and falling down like water squirting up from a fountain. His crazy feathers and his ducky smile make him look the epitome of silly goose.

"That's Lovey Bara, Maverick Limpright, and Bruce Goose respectively. We got all three of them fresh out of college this season. I've shown them what I can, and they're all pretty quick students of the game, but they're unpolished. They need a leader on the ice."

"Sure thing Coach." Rodman pauses a moment to think. "It looks like we've got lots of work to do."

"Indeed. But please call me Chip."

Rodman shoots Safari Chip a thumbs up.

*

Rodman and Safari Chip fly in over Las Vegas at night. From the sky, Las Vegas looks like a mega-sized amusement park made of state-of-the-art glow in the dark legos. The hotels are massive and vary in shapes from castles to pyramids to desert islands to palaces to upscale modern buildings, and they come in every color in the jumbo sized crayon box. Fountains and statues litter the streets. Billboards promote the world famous stage show acts of Ape Sinatra, Deer Martin, Froggy Davis Jr. and Elkvis Presley. The streets are crowded with cars, taxis, buses, and motorcycles. Plus, there are thousands of animals walking the Las Vegas Strip in every direction.

The plane lands at McCann International Airport. Inside the airport, Rodman is overwhelmed by all there is to see. Restaurants, gift shops, bookstores, and electronic stores line the hallways, and everywhere he looks, he sees slot machines, slot machines, and more slot machines. He's mesmerized at how different this airport is from the tiny one back home in South Africa. Occasionally, Rodman stops to look at something new to him, and Safari Chip has to drag him away from all the glitz.

In the baggage claim area, Safari Chip loses sight of Rodman. He panics as he looks around for his new star player. He runs around each of the baggage carousels looking for Rodman. He eventually catches a glimpse of the penguin out of the corner of his eye. Rodman sits atop his luggage, riding the carousel. Safari Chip puts his head in his hand and sighs.

Rodman hops off his bag and snatches it up. "Where to now Coach?"

"Now, we bring you to your new home. And stop calling me Coach. Call me Chip."

"Oh yeah. Chip."

They exit the airport and step to the passenger pick up curb where several taxis await.

"I'm a good whistler. Do you want me to hail us a taxi?" Rodman offers.

"Oh no, no, no, no my man. I told you, everything the Gamblers do, we do in style." Safari Chip whistles an ample whistle and motions to a waiting limo.

Rodman absolutely cannot believe his luck. Yesterday, he was walking around on foot. Today, he's riding around in limos. "Wow! If I'm riding around in limos, and I play for the last place team, I can only imagine the treatment Jason is getting in Alaska."

*

Jason sits on the side of the road outside the broken down bus. The tire change is slow-going. His face stings as he's unexpectedly nailed with a snowball. He spins his head towards two fox cubs frozen in fear staring back at him. Jason snarls at them, breaking their terrified trance.

They snarl back and spit their tongues out at him.

Unable to do anything about the attack, Jason goes back to minding his own business. He concentrates on how great life will be as a member of the Gold Rush. Suddenly, he's hit in the head with another snowball.

The cubs laugh and point.

Jason scoops up a snowball of his own, stands to peg the little buggers, but when he spins to fire, he's met by the sight of their father standing protectively in front of them.

Jason drops his snowball, puts his head down, and retreats to the other side of the street. Crossing the street he's almost run over by a Husky driving an eighteen-wheeler full of manure. The Husky slams hard on the brakes, but Jason still has to jump out of the way. He slams a fistful of flipper along the side of the truck as it pulls to a stop. "Hey! I'm walking here."

The Husky sticks his head out the window. "Sorry about that partner. I didn't see you coming from behind that there bus." He examines the bus. "You guys having some auto problems?"

"Flat tire," Jason says.

"Where you headed?"

"Anchorage."

"Hop in. I can get you there." The Husky motions for Jason to get in.

Jason shoots a sneer at the fox cubs before hopping in.

The cubs throw snowballs at the truck as it makes its retreat.

*

Rodman and Safari Chip ride in their limo down the Las Vegas Strip. Safari Chip sends some more text messages while Rodman stares out the window at all the buildings and neon signs. Sings that promote musical acts, dance shows, magic shows, pirate shows, circus acts, and impersonators. Other signs brilliantly flash the names of the hotels, names like The Kalahari, The Illusion, The Roman Palace, Hotel Tropical, Cala Luna Bay, The Chicago, Casablanca, and many more.

"Wow! Look at that!" Rodman, with his beak pressed against the window, points to the water show in front of the Fontana Hotel. His eyes glimmer with an overflow of excitement. "Oh wow! And look there." He points to a castle shaped hotel, the Hotel Camelot. His head whips around and his beak drops at a white hotel with pink trim and a mammoth pink neon sign shaped like a penguin. "They even have a hotel called The Pink Penguin!"

"That was the first ever hotel on the Strip," Safari Chip informs him.

"This is incredible. Where's the arena?"

"In the New Orleans Hotel."

"It's inside a hotel too?" Rodman asks.

"Everything is inside hotels here Rodman."

Rodman falls back into his seat and smiles. His mind races with the anticipation of surprises yet to come.

"It was a long flight. You must be hungry," Safari Chip says.

"And how."

"Your favorite dish is a fish sandwich, no?"

"Yes sir."

Safari Chip presses a button on his armrest. The button triggers a cooler to come up from a secret compartment. The lid of the cooler opens up to reveal a fish sandwich on a plate.

"Can I have that?"

"Of course my man!" Safari Chip hands the sandwich to Rodman.

"What about you?"

With the wink of an eye, Safari Chip presses another button on his panel, and a bushel of bananas comes out from another secret compartment.

"This is too much," Rodman says through a mouthful of sandwich.

A text comes through Safari Chip's phone, and he texts the sender back.

"You sure are a busy man."

"I'm just making sure some last minute arrangements have been completed." Safari Chip puts the phone back into his safari jacket.

They finish their meals as the limo pulls up to the New Orleans Hotel, an oversized hotel just like the ones on Bourbon Street. It's complete with tall stone arches on the first and second floors and wrought iron fences on the balconies. Street lamps surround the bottom level and there are large picture windows that climb into the sky thirty-five stories high. Rodman looks straight up at the building. It's so tall that it hurts to crane his neck so high. He looks back to Safari Chip and sees the monkey already entering the hotel. He rushes up the stairs that lead into the hotel to catch up with his coach.

They walk through a set of glass doors into a world of glimmer and sparkle the likes of which Rodman has never even dared to imagine. The abundance of slot machines inside the hotel puts the amount he saw at the airport to shame. They're all over the place, taking up almost every square inch of the entrance. The lobby is aglow underneath monstrous chandeliers made of long strands of diamond shaped glass jewels and flame shaped light bulbs.

The hotel is jamming. Rodman and Safari Chip make their way through the foyer, passing by roulette wheels, craps tubs, black jack and poker tables galore.

At different intervals, Rodman stops to stare at all the fun, but Safari Chip makes sure to keep him moving along. "Come on Rodman. We've got to get you checked in."

"Checked in?"

"Yep. This is where our players live during the season."

"We live here too!?"

Rodman and Safari Chip walk past a line of animals waiting to register. They make their way to an empty VIP line and head straight for a hotel employee. Safari Chip hands her some sort of official Gamblers card. She takes the card and swipes it through her computer. She looks up at Rodman with a coy smile. "Welcome to the New Orleans Mr. Penguin. It's a pleasure to have you."

"Thanks," Rodman replies.

She finishes up on her computer and hands Safari Chip two electronic door keys. He puts one in the pocket of his safari pants and hands the other to Rodman. They walk to an elevator room and wait for one of six elevators. A bell dings, the up arrow lights up, and the doors open.

"Good evening sirs." The elevator operator, Ed, an older but distinguished goat, greets them and steps aside to let them in. "Where to?"

"Thirty-fifth floor please," Safari Chip requests.

"Oh boy! The penthouse floor." Ed smiles a little wider, stands a little taller, and straightens his tie. He pushes the button marked thirty-five. He stands next to Safari Chip during the ride. He leans over, holds his hand over his mouth, and whispers, "Is he him sir?"

Rodman can hear his whisper.

Safari Chip mimics Ed's actions and whispers back, "He sure is."

Ed makes eye contact with Rodman. "It sure is good to have you on our team Mr. Penguin sir. Lord knows we could use a player like you. Not to mention all the help we can get!" Ed slaps his knee and laughs at his own awkward joke. He stops when he sees Rodman and Safari Chip don't join him. He straightens back up into a proper and upright position. "Don't get me wrong Mr. Rodman sir. These are good boys. They just need to smooth out the rough edges. Ain't that right Mr. Chip sir?"

"That's right Ed." Safari Chip looks to Rodman. "Ed comes to all the games."

"All of 'em," Ed reiterates. The elevator stops at the top floor and the bell rings. "Thirty-fifth floor! Penthouse!"

The doors open. Rodman and Safari Chip step out of the elevator. Rodman says good-bye to Ed, and Ed waves back. They step into a rather ordinary hallway. The carpet is tacky, mostly red with blue and green swirls and a smattering of yellow starry-type designs. The doors are plain beige with a puke green trim. The distance between each hotel room door indicates that the suites are substantial in size. They walk all the way to the end of the hallway where they finally reach room 3501.

Safari Chip puts his key card into a slot above the handle. The red light on the slot turns green, indicating that the door is unlocked. He opens the door for Rodman and reveals a world of excess luxury.

They step into Rodman's new home and immediately his beak drops. His home in South Africa was a tiny, one room tiki hut where the kitchen, dining room, bathroom, and living room were all visible from the front door. Before him now is a fully furnished suite that includes a sunken living room with a giant flat screen TV, a plush leather couch that seats ten, a desk with a laptop, and two very stylish lamps. Just past the living room is an enormous window with a view of the Las Vegas Strip. Outside, under the nighttime sky, the Strip sparkles and is alive with hustle and bustle.

Rodman runs from the front room to a hallway that goes left and right. He first takes a right and runs into his bedroom which includes a walk-in closet, private bathroom, hot tub, a bed built for a king, another flat screen TV, dresser, nightstand, empty book shelves, mini-fridge, another desk with a laptop, and a gift basket full of Gamblers merchandise. He sees the gift basket and runs to it but doesn't examine its contents. He gets distracted by the closet. He runs into and spins round and round inside then runs out and jumps into the empty hot tub.

Safari Chip watches from the doorway.

Rodman turns to him from inside the hot tub. "We've got to get this filled up!" He immediately jumps out of the tub, not waiting for a response. He runs out of the bedroom, back down the hallway, past the Strip view window, into the kitchen. "Wow! This is fantastic! I can't believe it."

"Well believe it," Safari Chip hollers from down the hallway.

Inside the kitchen with an adjacent dining room, there is a stove, dishwasher, microwave, and stainless steel refrigerator, all state of the art. Rodman opens the freezer to find it fully laden with fish packed on ice, and in the fridge is a wealth of water and passion fruit juice.

Safari Chip watches Rodman inspect the fridge. "We have the essentials in there, but if there's anything else you need or want, just let us know and we'll stock you up."

"This is so awesome!" Rodman runs out of the kitchen, back down the hallway towards his bedroom. He again runs right past the giant window with the Strip view, but this time he puts on the breaks. He walks slowly backwards to the window. He doesn't know how, but somehow he managed to miss this before. He presses himself against the center of the window and looks out upon his new hometown. "Wow!" he whispers. "If this is how a player on the last place team gets treated, I can only imagine how Jason is getting treated in Alaska!"

*

The Alaskan sky has grown dark. Jason and the Husky arrive outside a dumpy, rundown hotel in the middle of a small town. It's made of rickety, weathered, boards that wear a wilted paint job. The unstable sign mounted on the roof of the hotel reads First Class Inn, though it has been vandalized with the word Third spray painted over the word First.

Jason steps out of the big rig and takes a long hard look at the hotel in shock. *Prison likely has better living conditions.*

He's shocked again when he sees the bus he had been on earlier already parked in front of the hotel. *How could that have happened?*

Smelling like manure and in need of a bath, Jason neglects to thank the Husky for the ride. He walks up to the front door of the hotel and jiggles the handle, but it's locked. He pushes the door, but it doesn't budge. A sign on the door reads *Hotel Closed. Will Reopen At 7:00 A.M.*

Jason squawks loudly and bangs on the door.

*

Safari Chip stands with Rodman at his front door.

"What time is practice tomorrow Coach?"

"Ten in the morning sharp. And enough with the Coach business. Call me Chip!"

"Can I go and look around downstairs for a while Coa… Chip?"

"You can do whatever you want as long as you stay out of trouble and show up for practice and games on time."

"Oh boy!"

Rodman hops and clicks his heels. He runs out of his room, down the narrow hallway with its low ceilings and tacky carpet, leaving Safari Chip far behind. He rounds the corner to the elevator room and feverishly presses the button. He waits impatiently, pacing and playing with his flippers until the doors open, and he jumps back in with Ed.

*

After several minutes of Jason's pounding on the front door of his hotel, a light comes inside. A massive grizzly bear wearing a sleeping cap and a black robe comes to the door. He peers out the window and locks eyes with Jason. He growls,

"What do you mean banging on this door waking up all my guests?"

"I want in!" Jason growls back.

"Can't you read? We're closed."

"I know, but it's my first day in town. I was supposed to catch a bus here. It broke down. I hitched a ride with a manure truck. The bus still somehow beat me here. I have nowhere else to go. I'm tired. I'm hungry. And I want to come in and get comfortable in the room the Gold Rush reserved for me!" Jason throws his flippers up at the end of his tirade.

"Did you say the room the Gold Rush reserved for you?"

"Yeah."

The grizzly opens the door and steps aside. "You must be Jason Vyand. We were wondering what happened to you."

Jason walks into the dark hotel. He bumps his foot on a chair. "Ouch!"

"Just put your bags down anywhere. We'll have the staff bring them up to you in the morning." The grizzly grabs a room key behind the counter.

"I can bring them up myself."

"Suit yourself. I'm Frank by the way." He reaches his paw out to Jason.

With bags in both flippers, Jason awkwardly reaches for a clumsy shake.

Frank leads Jason up a rickety staircase and down an old fashioned hallway. The hotel has to be a hundred years old. They stop outside room number thirteen. Jason notes the ominous number. Frank opens the door and leads Jason into a room that could fit inside Rodman's closet. Sixty percent of the room is taken up by the tiny bed and very old dresser. The curtains are tacky and falling down, the bedding is old-fashioned, and the ten inch TV is set high upon a metal tray, chained to the wall, near the ceiling in the corner of the room. The bathroom is tucked away in a corner near the entrance.

"This is it?" Jason asks.

"Home sweet home," Frank says.

Jason drops his bags. He can't believe that a professional team, in any sport, would subject its star player to living conditions such as these. He vows to get himself a new place with his first Gold Rush paycheck.

*

Rodman jumps out of the elevator before the doors open all the way. He runs to a railing on a small platform. He looks around at all the hustle and bustle of the hotel with a mile wide grin. A hotel employee named Stan approaches Rodman and taps him on the shoulder.

Rodman spins around.

"Hello there," Stan greets him.

"Hi," Rodman says back.

"You must be Rodman T. Penguin."

"I am. How did you know?"

Stan points to a flashing, light bulb laden, framed poster on the wall behind Rodman. Inside the frame is a picture of Rodman while playing for the Chill. In the picture he skates with a puck right towards the camera. The poster reads: THE NEW ORLEANS HOTEL IS PROUD TO WELCOME THE NEWEST MEMBER OF THE LAS VEGAS GAMBLERS, RODMAN T. PENGUIN.

Rodman walks trancelike to the poster. He admires it for a long time. Not knowing the posters are what one of Safari Chip's numerous text messages were about, Rodman wonders where they got the picture, how they got it up so fast, and how much everyone has already been talking about him. He suddenly feels an overwhelming sense of duty to his new team and hometown. It makes him slightly nervous, but those feelings quickly give way to excitement.

"Oh wow," he whispers still staring at the poster. "If I'm playing for the last place team, and I'm getting posters, I can only imagine the advertisements they have for Jason in Alaska."

*

Ready for bed and deathly tired, Jason sits on his new bed. He lies down and notices an Alaska Gold Rush catalog with the current date on his bedside table. He eagerly opens it and goes right to the roster page to find his name. He finds that it isn't in there and slams the brochure into a wastebasket near the table. He pulls the covers over his head and goes to bed, hoping tomorrow will be a better day.

*

Stan interrupts Rodman as he stares at the poster. "Yes sir. We've all heard about you Mr. Penguin. And we're all mighty excited to see you play. Hopefully, you can turn this team around."

"I'm going to do my best," Rodman promises.

Stan throws a hoof around Rodman's shoulder. "Now let me clue you in on a few perks the Gamblers and the hotel have set up for you. All Gamblers eat free in any of the hotel's restaurants, you get limo rides where ever you need to go, and on your first night, we give you some free chips to play games inside the casino." Stan pulls a plastic rack full of colored playing chips from behind a podium as if he's been anticipating Rodman's arrival.

"Hot dog! I've never played any of these games before. What do you recommend?" Rodman asks.

"For a beginner?" Stan thinks. "You should try roulette. It's easy. You just bet on the numbers zero to thirty-six or the colors black, red, and green."

"Sounds easy enough," Rodman says.

Stan gives Rodman directions to the roulette tables. There, Rodman takes a seat at a table where the only other player is Sammie Lou, the Gamblers koala. Sammie is dressed in a white jacket, black shirt, black pants, and black sunglasses.

Neither recognizes the other. Unlike everyone else in the hotel, Sammie isn't suffering from Rod-mania.

"Hi," Rodman greets Sammie and the roulette dealer.

Slouching back in his seat, Sammie gives Rodman a nonchalant wave.

"Good evening sir," the dealer responds. "Place your bets please."

Sammie straightens up, leans over, and lays different colored chips all over the table.

Rodman watches Sammie, but he's hesitant to lay any of his own chips down. He's having too much fun just holding them and doesn't want to risk losing them.

Sammie sees Rodman's hesitation. "Have you never played before?"

"Nope. I don't quite know what to do," Rodman answers.

Still laying chips all over the board, Sammie explains to Rodman what Stan had gone over a minute ago. "Well you see, you put chips down on different numbers or colors. Then, the dealer spins the ball around in the wheel, and if your number or color comes up, you win."

"Oh." Rodman looks at the numbers on the board. "There's no number seventy-three?"

"No way. Only zero to thirty-six. Don't go giving the house any better odds by adding thirty-seven more numbers." Sammie continues placing his chips on the board.

"I really wanted to bet number seventy-three."

"Why seventy-three?"

"That's my number," Rodman beams.

"Oh. Well, you can bet number seven and number three if you'd like."

Rodman seems satisfied at that and places some black chips on seven and some blue chips on three. He also takes ten white chips and stacks them on the designated red square.

"Oh no, no, no. Don't ever bet red," Sammie warns Rodman as he places a stack of green chips twice the size of Rodman's red stack on the designated black square.

"Why?"

"It's one of those rules of life. Black just comes up more than red." Sammie lifts his glasses long enough to wink at Rodman, and then he lets them fall back upon his nose.

"But both seven and three are red numbers, and I bet them."

"Suit yourself." Sammie finishes laying down his chips. He sees that Rodman only has chips on three sections of the board. Meanwhile, he has about twenty-five different sections covered with chips. "Is that all you're going to bet?"

"Yep," Rodman answers.

"But you don't have a very good chance of winning my friend. Thirty-five other numbers can come up."

"It's ok. I feel lucky. Besides, like I said, seventy-three is my number."

The dealer spins the roulette wheel in one direction and sends the ball spinning on a track above the wheel in the opposite direction.

Sammie stares at Rodman. "That's twice you've said your number is seventy-three. What does that mean?"

"Oh. I just came here from South Africa to play hockey for the Gamblers. I wear number seventy-three." Rodman watches the ball spin around the top of the wheel.

"Rodman!? Rodman T. Penguin!?" Sammie stands from his chair.

"That's me." Rodman's gaze shifts from the wheel to Sammie.

"I didn't recognize you." Sammie makes his way to Rodman, grabs ahold of his flipper, and gives it a firm shake. "I'm Sammie Lou. Your right wing."

"Nice to meet you Sammie."

"Nice to meet you too Rod."

The roulette wheel winds down, the ball bounces a few times, and lands on number seven.

"Seven. Red. Winner," the dealer announces.

Sammie surveys the board. He sighs. "Ugh! I didn't have red or seven."

"That's a bummer," Rodman says.

"But hey man, you did! You had red and seven." Sammie points out Rodman's winning sections on the board.

"I told you I was feeling lucky."

The dealer takes the losing chips off the board. Then, she counts out and pushes two hundred and ten black chips and twenty white chips Rodman's way for picking the right number and color.

"Wow!" yells Sammie. "Look how many chips you won."

"Hot dog! I wasn't expecting to win that much." Rodman reaches for his chips.

Sammie takes in a deep breath and sighs once more. "Well, that's it for me. I'm off to the Mardi Gras Room."

"The Mardi Gras Room?" Rodman asks.

"Yeah! It's a place inside the hotel where they play music, there's dancing, food, and plenty of good times. You should come with me."

"It sounds fun, but it's already kind of late, and we have practice early in the morning. How late do you plan to stay there?"

"Oh I don't know. Sometimes until daybreak," Sammie says.

The wheels in Rodman's head turn full speed. *Isn't Sammie the one who always shows up to practice half asleep? Could it be because he's out too late the night before?* Rodman doesn't want to jump to any conclusions, but he's no fool. "Maybe another time. I want to be fresh for my first practice."

"Ok man. See you tomorrow."

"Sure thing." Rodman watches Sammie walk away.

"Any more bets?" the dealer asks him.

Rodman turns back to her. "Not for me tonight. But thanks. I had a good time. And here's for you." Rodman puts a stack of black chips on the three square. "I feel good about this spin. You can have whatever it wins."

"Thank you sir." The dealer spins the wheel and the ball.

"Do you know where in here is the best place to eat?"

"What do you like to eat?" she asks.

"I could really go for a fish sandwich."

"You should try The Gulf Grill. They have a wide variety of seafood."

"Thanks."

"Any time Rodman T. Penguin." She flashes him a mischievous smile.

"Wow! Does everybody know me?"

"You're already a pretty big deal around here. We haven't had a good team in a long time, and we're dying to see our Gamblers have a good year for a change."

Rodman feels that overwhelming sense of obligation again. "I promise I'm going to do everything I can to turn this team around. I better get going though if I'm going to get a sandwich before bed." He waves to her and walks towards The Gulf Grill.

The ball bounces into the roulette wheel as he's walking away. It lands on three. Even in the noisy casino, Rodman can hear her excited screams behind him, and it makes him smile. He grabs a fish sandwich and takes it back to his room where he devours it and hops into bed, eager to fall asleep and get rested for his first practice as a Gambler.

Chapter 5: First Gamblers Practice

Rodman can't fight off his eagerness to get to his first Gamblers practice even while he sleeps. He tosses and turns and wakes up long before his alarm goes off. In an effort to pass the time, he whips up a hearty fish omelet breakfast, moves the dining room table over to his large window, and eats while enjoying the view of his new city. It looks quite different in the daytime. It's not half as busy. Breakfast flies by, leaving Rodman with a few hours still to fill before practice. He tries to stay occupied, but the seconds move more like minutes.

A sudden knock at his door startles him. He waddles to answer it, but no one's there. Hanging on the outside handle, encased in plastic wrapping, is his practice jersey. He brings the uniform in and tears off the plastic. He holds up the plain white jersey. The only color on it at all is the logo on the chest, a replica of the Las Vegas welcome sign at the edge of the Strip. Two hockey sticks run through the logo to form an X and GAMBLERS is spelled out in alternating red and black letters along the bottom. The back of his jersey bears his first name in red and the number seventy-three in black with red and gold shadowing. Plain as it is, Rodman still jumps into it with a fervor. He races to the nearest mirror and gives himself a once over. Just the look and the feel of the jersey makes him excited. He's a member of the Las Vegas Gamblers. He's a true professional hockey player.

He gathers his equipment and rushes out of his room, down the elevator, to the lobby, and makes his way to the arena. With nothing better to do, he arrives for practice over an hour early. He loosens up by doing some light skating around the ice and shooting pucks at an empty net. While lining up some pucks, he hears a rumbling from the tunnel that leads from the locker room to the ice. He looks to the tunnel as the rumbling gets louder and closer.

One by one, the Gamblers appear at the tunnel exit. They stop when they see Rodman. There's a brief uncomfortable stare down between Rodman and his new teammates. The silence makes his heart leap into his throat. He knows he's the new guy, and he knows how the new guy usually gets treated. Just as he's about to jump out of his feathers with uneasiness, all the Gamblers scream with joy and skate to him as fast as they can.

Liten reaches him first. He grabs Rodman's flipper and shakes it. "You must be Rodman T. Penguin. It is sure nice to meet you. I am Liten Mus," says the mouse with a German accent.

"I'm Lovey Bara," says the teddy bear.

"Keith Kane. I'm on defense," says the Shih Tzu.

"You can call me Undertaker," says the other dog.

"I'm Maverick Limpright," says the horse.

"Bruce Goose," says the goose.

"Hi. I'm Harlan T. Turtle," says the turtle hiding at the back of the group.

Rodman notices Sammie is inauspiciously missing. He hopes this isn't a sign of things to come. He also hopes it doesn't have anything to do with Sammie's trip to the Mardi Gras Room last night. "Hi. It's great to meet you all. I can't tell you guys how excited I am to be a part of this team."

Everyone hoots and hollers.

"So, how do our practices usually work?" Rodman asks.

"Normally, we work on our biggest issue from the previous game," Liten answers.

"Oh. And what was the biggest problem during your last game?" Rodman asks.

"We were out on the ice playing hockey," jokes Undertaker. He and Kane laugh heartily.

"Normally, we wait for Chip to get here before we start," Harlan says with his flippers held behind his shell, looking bashfully towards the ice.

"Well, I don't want to come in and start changing anything, but perhaps we can all do some simple drills before the coach gets here?"

There's a unanimous agreement amongst the Gamblers.

"What do you want us to do?" Lovey asks.

"We can start with…" Rodman interrupts himself. "Hey. Where's Sammie?"

Undertaker and Kane laugh as though they've just heard the world's funniest joke.

"Where's Sammie?" Kane asks sarcastically. "Let me tell you something bro. We'll be lucky if Sammie shows up at all."

Rodman frowns.

"Sammie usually comes halfway through practice. If he comes at all," Harlan explains.

"And usually, he is not even able to finish half a practice," Liten adds.

Rodman groans. "Well, let's start without him. We can start with a passing drill."

Rodman lines up half the team along one side of the boards and the other half along the other side. He takes the puck and passes it across the ice to Liten. They pass the puck back and forth as they skate towards each other. Each pass gets shorter and quicker until they pass each other. Rodman skates to the back of the line on his new side, and the drill repeats with Liten and Lovey. The first three skaters, Rodman, Liten, and Lovey, all do fairly well, but it's apparent that the rest are in desperate need of some basic skill developing.

The Gamblers are eager to practice though, and they're so engrossed in the drill that they don't see Safari Chip approach them. At his whistle, they all look up and line up in front of him.

"Good morning team. It looks like you've already met Rodman, but let me formally introduce you guys to our newest player." Safari Chip, no longer in a suit, but a Gamblers windbreaker, black athletic pants, and his safari hat, puts his arm around Rodman, and brings him in front of the team. "This is Rodman T. Penguin. He's come to us by way of the South African Hockey League where he was the best player on the best team."

There's a collection of excited oooh's and ahhh's.

"Ok. Ok. Ok. Calm down everyone. Rodman's going to..."

"You were the best player on the best team?" Undertaker interrupts.

"And you want to play for *this* team?" Kane asks.

"Well, to be honest, I had a really bad game the night the Gold Rush scout came to see me play, and this was the only contract I could get," Rodman answers.

The Gamblers groan with disappointment.

Realizing his words might not have come out right, Rodman recovers quickly. "But that's not to say I don't want to play for this team. I do very much. It's always been my dream to play in the IAHL, no matter the team."

"Rodman was sabotaged by an inferior teammate the night I went to scout him. Luckily, the Gold Rush signed that guy, and we got Rodman." Safari Chip explains.

"And from what I've heard from Coach..." Rodman starts.

"Chip," Safari Chip interrupts.

"Chip," Rodman continues. "This is a really good team that just has a few kinks."

"Sure," Undertaker says sarcastically.

"Yeah, if by *a few* kinks you mean a ton," Kane chuckles.

"Seriously, when I started with the Chill, we weren't always so good. We certainly weren't the best. But, with some hard work, practice, and really good game planning, we turned things around."

"That's true," Safari Chip assures them. "And, it's because of Rodman's ability to help us learn and be a leader on the ice that I've decided to appoint him captain."

Rodman's humbled and a little embarrassed. It's not customary for the new guy to step in and take over the captain's role. That's usually reserved for someone who's been on the team for many years. No one seems upset though. They trust

Safari Chip's judgment. Though not always the best players on the ice, they're the epitome of the word team in all other facets.

"Let's go show Rodman what we've got, and then he can show us a thing or two." Safari Chip blows his whistle and the Gamblers skate past him towards center ice. He counts only eight players as they skate by. Without running down the roster he knows who's missing. "Anyone know where Sammie is?"

"Late again Coach," answers Harlan.

Safari Chip joins his players at center ice. "We'll start without him. So we lost our last game by a score of 14-0. I'm not sure if our biggest problem was defense and goaltending or the lack of offense, but I thought we'd start today's practice with a little of both. Let's start with a shooting drill, and we'll have Harlan try to block the shots."

The Gamblers line up side by side in front of the net. Each player has a pile of pucks in front of him. Harlan stands in front of the net in full pads. At Safari Chip's whistle, the players start shooting their pucks at the net. Harlan ducks his head in and out of his shell when the pucks come even remotely close to him.

With their last puck, each player takes a turn skating at Harlan for a moving shot. Rodman shoots last. He rears back and fires, sending not only Harlan's head but all four of his limbs into his shell. Harlan's left spinning on the ice as the puck whizzes past him into the back of the net.

Rodman skates to Safari Chip's side. Both look distressed.

"You ok Harlan?" Rodman calls.

"I'm fine," Harlan replies from inside his shell.

"Do you want to come out of your shell any time soon?" Safari Chip asks.

"I suppose I could." Harlan slowly pokes his head and the rest of his limbs out.

Rodman skates to Harlan. "I couldn't help but notice that you looked a little scared when we were shooting at you."

"You can say it. I was a lot scared." Harlan looks down at the ice humiliated.

"Can I ask how come? I mean, you've got a ton of padding on."

"I know, but the idea of a frozen piece of rubber hitting me, padding or not, scares the shell out of me," Harlan confesses.

Rodman puts his flipper to his beak and thinks. "Have you ever been hit with a puck?"

"Well yeah. All the time."

"I mean really hit! Not just grazed by one or had one bounce off of you accidently," Rodman clarifies.

"Oh. Well. No. Not really."

At the other end of the ice, the arena doors open and slam shut. Everyone turns to see Sammie trudging sluggishly in. He makes his way to the team still wearing the clothes he was wearing the night before. "Hey guys. Sorry I'm late."

Safari Chip shakes his head disapprovingly and makes some notes on his clipboard. "You're always sorry Sammie. Why can't you ever be on time?"

"I'll make sure to do better tomorrow Chip," Sammie promises insincerely.

"Where are your skates?" Safari Chip asks.

"I figured since I was already late I better get here as soon as I could, so I skipped the skates today. I can just practice in my shoes. I'll get them..."

"You'll get them now," Safari Chip cuts Sammie off and motions to the locker room with his thumb. "And put on a jersey and pads while you're at it."

Sammie grunts and mumbles something indiscernible as he makes the short trek from the ice to the locker room. With the distracting koala gone, all attention goes back to Rodman and Harlan.

"Harlan, if I show you that it doesn't hurt, do you think you could give it a try without ducking into your shell?" Rodman asks.

Harlan shrugs. "Maybe."

Rodman skates to the team bench and throws on an extra set of goalie equipment. He pats Harlan on the shell as he skates past him on his way to the net. "Ok buddy. Watch this." He takes his place in front of the net. "Ok guys. Let me have it."

Liten, Lovey, Maverick, and Goose line up in front of Rodman with a pile of pucks in front of each player. Sammie returns in the proper skates and hockey attire and joins the line, but he struggles to keep his eyes open. Safari Chip blows his whistle, and the pucks start flying at Rodman. Most of the shots are spot on, though Sammie's shots have no zip to them. Rodman lets the pucks hit him all over the chest protector, helmet, gloves, and leg pads. Harlan watches amazed as Rodman jumps into the way of each shot until the other players run out of pucks.

Rodman takes off his mask. Smiling roguishly he asks his team, "Is that all you guys got? Where are the big hitters?"

As an answer to his question, Undertaker and Kane skate into view in front of him. Maverick and Goose dump a new pile of pucks in front of each dog.

"So you guys are the big sticks?" Rodman pulls his mask down and digs back in. "Show me what you've got."

Safari Chip blows his whistle again. The dogs start shooting. Each shot is one thunderous blast after another. Rodman stands his ground, taking the hard shots off his pads and helmet. Occasionally, he even catches a shot with his glove and flips it away while he blocks other pucks with his stick or his leg.

"We should make him our goalie," Lovey whispers to Safari Chip.

Undertaker and Kane run out of pucks, and Rodman removes his mask again. He skates back to Harlan and throws his flipper around the turtle.

"That was cool," Harlan says.

"See. All those blasts, and I'm fine. Want to give it another try?"

"Yeah," Harlan eagerly agrees. He skates back to the net and digs in.

Rodman grabs Liten and Lovey. They line up in front of a fresh pile of pucks. Rodman nods to Harlan, asking if he's ready.

Harlan nods back.

Rodman gives Safari Chip a thumbs up. The coach blows his whistle, and the three players bombard Harlan with pucks. Immediately, the turtle jumps back into his shell, and all the pucks go right past him into the net. Harlan falls so hard and so fast that he's left spinning on his shell again.

Safari Chip blows his whistle before the three shooters run out of pucks.

The Gamblers stop shooting.

Harlan pokes his head out of his shell just enough to see his coach's eyes. "Sorry."

"It's ok. You just need more practice," Safari Chip says.

"Why don't you guys keep practicing? I have to talk to Coach about something." Rodman grabs Safari Chip, and they make their way to the bench while the Gamblers continue to shoot at Harlan.

"Coach, I don't want…"

"Chip."

"Sorry. Chip, I don't want to tell you how to run your team, but I do have a suggestion."

"I'm all ears," Safari Chip says.

"I think you need to enforce a curfew."

"A curfew?"

"Yeah. A time in which all players should be home and in bed."

"I know what a curfew is Rodman, but do you really think it's necessary?"

"I don't want to name names, but I think there might be someone on the team who is staying out way too late, doing things that are detrimental to his hockey play."

"Really!? Who?" Safari Chip spins around and surveys his team.

Not wanting to be a complete rat, Rodman shrugs but in the same motion uses his head to point out Sammie, who is literally asleep on his feet. The only thing keeping the koala from falling is that he's leaning against his stick as he sleeps.

Safari Chip spots Sammie. "That's not a bad idea Rodman, but what about the other players? I don't want to punish everyone because one of them is messing up."

"It's not a punishment, and I don't think they'll mind too much anyway. It won't hurt to make sure everyone is rested and ready to go. And, I'll bet that with a curfew in effect, a rested and ready Sammie Lou will return to all-star form."

"You're pretty smart Rodman. You've got lots of good ideas." Safari Chip puts Rodman in a playful headlock and gives him noogies.

Rodman laughs as he's rough-housed.

"I'm glad we got you and not the Gold Rush. Oh, and speaking of the Gold Rush. We play them next."

Rodman's demeanor turns serious. "In that case, we better get back to practicing."

*

The Gold Rush hold a very rigid practice in their arena. Jason fits right in with their machinelike style. He and the other players skate from their blue line towards pucks that have been set on the ice. They take shots at their goalie with no more instruction than a whistle blown by Coil as he slithers along the ice.

Jason skates from the front of the line to the shooting line. Around his neck is Rodman's lucky scarf. He approaches the puck, scoops it up, and races towards his goalie. He hits the puck with such aggression that it whizzes past the lightning quick hare so fast he doesn't even have time to flinch. The puck sails past Haas into the net.

Jason smiles arrogantly, and Coil matches his malevolent grin.

Haas removes his goalie mask. He and the other Gold Rush players stare at Jason intimidated. They all share the same thought. They're just glad he's on their team and they don't have to face him.

Chapter 6: Gamblers vs. The Gold Rush Game One

In his ever so comfy new bed, Rodman tosses and turns. He wakes up in the middle of the night to find his mouth totally dried out. Dying for a drink, he crawls out of bed and heads for his kitchen. He grabs an ice cube tray from the freezer and tries to empty some ice into his glass. He shakes and shakes and shakes the tray, but nothing comes out. Finally, he flips on a light and looks into an empty tray. He sighs and drops the ice cube tray, grabs the hotel ice bucket, and heads for the front door. As he walks to the door, he notes the time on the clock in his living room, 1:16 a.m.

As quick as he exits his room, he jumps back in when he sees his neighbor, Sammie, poking his head out of his own room. Sammie doesn't appear to have seen Rodman, so Rodman carefully peeks back into the hall in time to see Sammie, dressed for a night on the town, sneak out past curfew. Rodman knows this isn't going to be good for Sammie or the rest of the team come tomorrow. He sighs again and waits for Sammie to round the corner that leads to the elevator room. Once he's sure Sammie is gone, Rodman proceeds to the ice maker.

*

In the Gamblers locker room, Rodman can't sit still. He's raring to go and can barely stand the wait for his debut. He paces back and forth from his locker to a mirror, stopping to admire himself in his new, official, Gamblers game day jersey. This jersey is much more decorative than his practice jersey. It's black with red trim on the shoulders, wrists and at the bottom. The Red is then outlined in gold. A pair of colliding red dice with the letters L and V instead of white dots serve as the logo on the chest. Unlike the rest of the team, Rodman's jersey bears a red captain's C near his heart. On the back of the jersey, RODMAN is spelled out in all capital red letters, and the number seventy-three is white outlined in red and gold. On the bottom left corner of the back is a small print of the Las Vegas Sign.

While pacing, Rodman continually greets, high fives, or acknowledges his teammates in one way or another. He does this so many times he starts to annoy some of them. For the third time, he passes Liten and asks, "Hey Liten. You feeling good? You ready?"

Liten squints. "Rodman?"

"Yeah?"

"That is the third time in the last three minutes you have asked if I am ready. I am ready."

"Oh. Sorry. I'm just kind of excited." Rodman smiles nervously.

Behind them, Safari Chip comes out of his office. He looks around the locker room and counts his players. As always, he's down one player. He sighs as he drops and shakes his head in the same motion. He stares at the ground for a moment, thinking about what to do about Sammie. "Ten minutes to game time. Has anyone seen Sammie?"

There's a collective silence around the room.

"That darn koala is going to be the death of me."

As the last word escapes Safari Chip's mouth, the locker room doors swing open and Sammie, still wearing his clothes from the night before, lumbers into the room. All heads turn to him. Safari Chip shoots Sammie an extremely irritated and disappointed look. Sammie doesn't notice. He slumps across the room and plops into the chair in front of his locker.

Rodman sees the agitation on Safari Chip's face and walks over to him. "Can I have a word with you in private Coach?"

So irritated with Sammie, Safari Chip doesn't notice Rodman call him Coach. "Sure Rodman. Step into my office."

Safari Chip seems distracted even in his office. He paces around in short half circles and mumbles indiscernibly.

Rodman grabs his coach by the shoulders and leads him to the seat usually reserved for players. "Relax Coach. Let's talk."

"What's up Rodman?"

"I don't want to be a snitch, but I saw Sammie leave his room after curfew last night."

"You're no snitch. It's clear as day he's been out all night." Safari Chip stands back up and flails his arms all over the place.

"He's not going to do the team any good if he's asleep on the ice."

"I know," Safari Chip agrees. "I guess the only thing to do is to suspend him."

"That might not be a bad idea. It should be a wakeup call to him."

Safari Chip mulls the situation over in his head, going back and forth over and over his options. He doesn't want to suspend Sammie. Without him, everyone will have to play more, and that means they'll get worn out quicker. On the other hand, he wants to teach Sammie about consequences. Plus, if Sammie's asleep on the bench, the other guys will still have to fill in for him. After going round and round with himself, he makes a decision. "Do me a favor Rodman. Send Sammie in here. Then lead the rest of the team to the ice."

"Can do Coach." Rodman exits the office. He makes his way to Sammie, who snores loudly in his chair. Rodman puts a flipper on Sammie's shoulder and shakes him, but the koala doesn't stir, so Rodman shakes harder.

Sammie wakes up, but just barely. "Hey Rodman."

"Hey man. Coach wants to see you."

Sammie groans and stares at Rodman annoyed for a moment. He doesn't appreciate his nap being interrupted, but even though he struggles, he pulls himself out of his chair, and slogs his way into Safari Chip's office without knocking.

Rodman calls to the rest of the team, "Ok guys let's hit the ice."

The Gamblers rush for the locker room exit.

*

Rodman and the Gamblers wait in the tunnel just outside the ice for their introductions. The arena is sold out. The crowd is extra rowdy, and the noise from their clapping, shouting, horns, cowbells, noise makers, mega phones, and clackers is deafening. Rodman's awestruck at the energy coming from each and every one of the crazy animals in attendance. Through red, white, and gold spotlights that circle around the darkened arena, Rodman can tell that almost everyone is wearing a Gamblers jersey or t-shirt. Some even already have Rodman t-shirts and jerseys.

In a monotone voice, the arena announcer finishes the Gold Rush introductions to loud boos from the Gamblers fans. They boo all opponents, but they especially hate the Gold Rush.

Suddenly, the announcer roars to life, and the speakers boom. *"And now, it's time to introduce your Las Vegas Gamblers!"*

The crowd goes nuts.

"Starting in goal, number twenty, *Harlan T. Turtle!*"

Harlan rushes out of the tunnel under the glow of a golden spotlight. His picture and stats appear on the jumbo screen above the ice. The crowd goes crazy, clapping, stomping, and cheering.

"Starting on defense, number thirteen, *Morty "Undertaker" Curtains!*"

Undertaker takes the ice next underneath the golden spotlight. The picture and stats on the jumbo screen change to his as they do with every introduction. Undertaker does laps around Harlan and the Gamblers net.

"Also starting on defense, number ninety-nine, *Keith Kane!*"

Kane skates out underneath the golden spotlight and joins Undertaker as the noise of the crowd continues to grow.

Rodman shivers waiting for his name to be called.

"Starting at left wing, number seventeen, *Liten Mus!*"

Liten skates out, taking huge strides with his tiny legs. The golden spotlight follows him as he skates in between Undertaker and Kane. The tiny mouse gives each of the larger dogs a few bumps to pump them up, and they bump him back.

"Starting at right wing, number sixteen, *Lovey Bara!*"

Lovey skates out for the first time under the glow of the golden spotlight reserved for starters. He joins the others in their moshing.

Rodman's heart beats faster. He knows he's next.

"*And now!*" The announcer bellows with even more enthusiasm.

The crowd already knows what's coming. They get louder, stomping on the bleachers and kicking away at their seats.

The announcer pauses to let the anticipation grow.

It's almost too much for Rodman to handle. He takes a deep breath and gets a tickle in his lungs as they try to process the oxygen. Under his feathers, he has goosebumps and unsettled nerves.

"Introducing for the first time in the IAHL, and for the first time as a member of the Las Vegas Gamblers, starting at center, he wears number seventy-three, *your new* team captain, the one, the only, *Rodman T. Penguin!*"

Rodman is on the ice at the mention of his first name. Almost impossible to think, but the crowd grows even louder. The entire arena is absolutely deafening as he comes out of the tunnel. The spotlight hits him, illuminating his happy-go-lucky smile enough for every one of the 30,573 patrons in attendance to see. Safari Chip knew the games were going to be sold out almost every night with Rodman on the team, so he had a construction team cram an extra seventy-three seats into the arena in honor of Rodman.

Rodman is so excited that everything becomes a blur and the noise of the crowd drowns out. He can't even see his teammates as he skates right next to them, and he hears only silence.

Maverick and Goose are introduced as the backups and make their way to the bench. Safari Chip is also introduced, but he fails to come out of the tunnel as he's still dealing with Sammie in the locker room.

The lights come up but only slightly, and the starters for each team stand on their blue line under their own red, white, or blue spotlight for the American National Anthem.

Rodman's smile remains cemented on his face. He takes in every sight and tries to hold onto every second of his debut. He knows he'll only have one, and he wants it to last as long as possible, and he doesn't want to forget anything about it.

The anthem ends and the lights come up all the way.

To Rodman, the ice seems extra white, the lights extra bright, and the overall feel is bigger than anything he's ever experienced. He and the rest of the Gamblers do laps around Harlan and the net as they wait for Safari Chip.

The referees notice Safari Chip's absence and give the Gamblers some extra time. Eventually, they have to get the game underway, and one of the referees skates to the Gamblers. "Hey guys. Where's your coach?"

Rodman looks nervously to the tunnel. Luckily, Safari Chip comes out, alone, at just that moment. Rodman points to him. "There he is."

The referee blows his whistle and raises his arm. "Ok. Let's play."

Rodman skates to center ice for the faceoff. He lines up across from Jason.

"Rodman?" Jason asks as though he doesn't recognize him. "Is that you?"

"Hey Jason," Rodman says unable to conceal his anger.

"What are *you* doing here?"

"I'm playing with the Gamblers." Rodman doesn't appreciate Jason's mocking manner.

"The worst team in the league eh? I guess after that last game back home you were lucky to even make that team."

"I know what you did." Rodman digs in.

"Oh yeah?" Jason digs in too.

"Yeah."

The referee moves in between the penguins. He leans in, looks each of them in the eye, and raises the puck for only a second before he lets it drop. Rodman drives a shoulder into Jason, bumps him backwards, swipes the puck with his stick, and wins the faceoff. Jason tries to retaliate, but Rodman pushes him down to the ice with a thud and goes to join his team on offense.

Kane takes the puck across the blue line. One of the Gold Rush players, Iggy Jarrett, a Marine Iguana from the Galapagos Islands, skates towards Kane and forces him to pass the puck.

Liten corrals the puck and skates towards the net. One of the Gold Rush defensemen, Aaron Packer, a black and white cat, leaps in his way and bears his razor sharp teeth. Liten drops his stick, covers his face, and loses the puck.

Packer passes the puck to Mike Metz, an orange and black cat. Metz changes directions and takes the puck back towards Harlan, skating near the glass on his way. He's stopped abruptly by Undertaker, who jumps with both feet off the ice and smashes Metz violently against the glass. The cat's eyes bulge from his head like they're going to pop out. He falls limply to the ice and remains on his back. Undertaker lands beside him but gets up quickly with a grin a mile wide.

The crowd goes nuts, and Undertaker nods to his cheering fans, but a whistle blows and play stops. One of the referees makes a signal indicating a boarding penalty. Boarding is when a player viciously smashes an opposing player into the boards in a potentially dangerous manner, usually head first or from behind.

"Boarding. Number thirteen. Las Vegas. Five minutes," the referee announces.

Undertaker whips around at the referee's voice and skates at him. He's confused as he always is when getting called for a penalty. "Awww come on now! What are you talking about?"

"That was a dirty hit Morty." The referee skates away from Undertaker.

Undertaker gives chase. "It's Undertaker. Not Morty."

"Five minutes!" The referee points to the penalty box.

"No way! Come on ref!" Undertaker continues to follow him and plead his case.

Rodman intercepts the unruly dog. "Wait Undertaker. Just go sit in the box for five minutes. We don't need you to get a misconduct penalty too."

"But I didn't do anything wrong." Undertaker truly doesn't understand what his mistake was.

Rodman puts his flipper around Undertaker and skates him to the penalty box where an attendant is waiting with the door opened. Undertaker goes inside and slams his helmet on the bench as Rodman skates back to center ice.

Metz skates past the penalty box with a devilish grin. He taps the glass with his stick and hisses, causing the dog to jump and bark at the glass.

The Gamblers, with only four players, head to the faceoff on the penalty kill. Rodman and Jason don't speak as they faceoff this time.

The referee drops the puck.

Jason wins.

Packer brings the puck over the blue line and starts a succession of quick passes from one Gold Rush to another. The speed and crispness of their passing is a sight to see. The Gamblers take to a formation known as the diamond defense. It works for a while, but the passes of the Gold Rush get quicker and trickier.

Lovey and Kane begin to lose ground on Metz and Packer. Liten holds his own for a while against Rapture, a vulture, but suddenly Rapture and Metz switch positions. Metz growls at Liten, causing the mouse to once again cower and be taken out of the play.

Metz leaves the cowering mouse and joins Iggy. Together, they create a wall in front of Rodman, allowing Jason to make a move around him. Rodman tries to chase Jason, but he bumps into the pick set by other Gold Rush players. From behind the Gold Rush defenders, Rodman can see Harlan trembling as Jason moves in and rears back to take his shot.

Lovey sees the play breaking down too, and he rushes away from Packer towards Jason. He bumps Jason, disrupting his shot attempt and diverting him away from the net.

The interruption gives Rodman more time. He pushes past Metz and Iggy, but Jason reestablishes himself before Rodman can get to him.

Jason rears back to fire the puck at the net.

Rodman knows he's not going to be able to reach Jason in time to disrupt his shot, so he races for the front of the net instead.

Even before the sound of the stick hitting the puck, Harlan hides in his shell.

Rodman dives, horizontal to the ice, just in time to fly in front of the puck. He blocks the shot for Harlan, but he pays a price when he lands with a thud and has his wind knocked out.

The puck is sent backwards and collected by Kane. He quickly passes it to Liten and the mouse skates hastily to the other end of the ice.

Behind Liten, players from both teams give chase, including Packer, who speeds towards him with his fangs out. His freshly sharpened claws pop out of his glove, and he raises one of his paws. As he gains ground on Liten, Packer arches his back and curls back his lips to reveal even more bladelike teeth. Just as he's about to demolish Liten, Kane comes in and spins Packer around with the curved end of his stick. Packer turns around with a look of shock and awe, but he doesn't even have time to raise his paws in self defense before Kane uses his stick to smash him under the jaw. The hit sends the cat flying backwards and falling to the ice.

Behind the play, a whistle blows and play stops. The referee indicates more penalties. The first is a hooking penalty, which is when someone uses their stick to impede the progress of another player. The second is a cross checking penalty, which is when a player uses the shaft of the stick to forcefully hit an opponent.

"There are several infractions on the play. Hooking. Number ninety-nine. Las Vegas. Two minutes. Cross checking. Number ninety-nine. Las Vegas. Two minutes," the referee announces.

Kane can't believe the call. In his mind, he was saving his teammate from being diced up. "Oh come on ref. You've got to be kidding me!"

Rodman skates to Kane and drags him to the penalty box. The attendant opens the door for Kane. Before he can shut it again, Undertaker joins Kane at the door.

"Rodman. You've got to do something. These refs are totally against us," Undertaker complains.

"Yeah. We didn't do anything wrong," Kane barks.

"Actually guys, you did. Do you even know the rules of hockey?" Rodman asks.

"Yeah." Undertaker looks insulted.

"Of course," Kane asserts.

"What are they?" Rodman quizzes.

"You hit the other players and take the puck," Undertaker starts.

"Then you shoot the puck into the net. That's how you win," Kane finishes.

"But there's so much more. You can't just smash the other player as hard as you can whenever you want. Nor can you hit them with your stick," Rodman says.

"We get hit all the time though," Kane argues.

"There's a difference between hitting and... It's..." Rodman shakes his head. "We'll go over it tomorrow in practice."

A referee comes up behind Rodman. "Rodman, let's go."

Rodman turns back to the dogs. "I have to go. Just do me a favor."

"Sure," Undertaker says.

"When you come back out on the ice, try to tone the violence down," Rodman begs.

Both dogs roll their eyes and chuckle. Tone down the violence? Not a chance.

"Ok Hott Rod," Kane mocks.

"Anything you say Mr. Penguin," Undertaker laughs.

Rodman sighs and leaves the dogs. He skates to center ice for another faceoff. The Gamblers remain on the penalty kill, but they now have only three players on the ice. Lovey and Liten take a seat on the bench and are replaced by the fresh legs of Maverick and Goose.

The puck drops, and the faceoff is won by Jason.

The game goes on and on this way. Jason wins faceoff after faceoff as Rodman grows increasingly tired from playing so much of the game on the penalty kill. Liten gets continually destroyed by the cats. Undertaker and Kane pile up the penalty minutes as they brutalize anyone who steps on the ice for Alaska. The Gold Rush players limp, crawl, and are carried off the ice in pain. Jason scores a goal, and then another, and then a third for what is known in hockey as a hat trick. The Gold Rush score again and again with Harlan ducking into his shell every time they shoot. The crowd boos. Rodman does his best to get the Gamblers on the board, but all of his shots are stopped by Haas. At one point, Rodman takes a shot and gets two instantaneous rebounds, but Haas manages to block all three shots. Maverick and Goose try to defend against the Gold Rush offense, but they end up running into each other over and over. With the referee's backs to the play, Jason and Iggy skate up behind Rodman and use their sticks to take his legs out from underneath him. Eventually, fed up with getting hit, clawed, and defiled, Liten uses his stick as a weapon to slash both of his cat attackers so he can go to the only place where he knows he'll be safe, the penalty box. Undertaker, Kane, and Liten sit in the penalty box together. Up to four players can fit in the penalty box at one time, but only two players at a time can serve their penalty.

The final score is 9-0, Gold Rush over the Gamblers. Rodman is forced to watch Jason and the Gold Rush celebrate their victory on his new home ice, the night of his grand debut. He and the rest of the Gamblers skate off the ice worn out, beat up, and downtrodden.

The Gamblers file into their locker room with their heads hung low. They're deflated.

Sammie sits with his arms folded on a table near his locker. He watches his teammates as they lumber in and head for a seat near their locker. When he sees Rodman, he makes eye contact and directs an angry glare his way.

Safari Chip stands at the forefront of the silent room. Everyone can feel his gaze, but no one looks at him. "We got crushed out there guys," he says, breaking the silence.

"No duh!" Kane mumbles.

"And do you know why we got crushed?" Safari Chip directs the question at the wisecracking dog.

"Because the Gold Rush cheated?" Kane offers a guess.

"Because the other team was on the power play for fifty-seven minutes?" Liten guesses.

"Because they're better skaters, shooters, and puck handlers?" Lovey offers yet another.

"Because they're the best team in the league?" Undertaker adds a fourth.

"No! Well, kind of because they're the best team, but do you know the only reason they're better than us?" Safari Chip asks.

"Skill?" Undertaker guesses.

"Talent?" guesses Kane.

"Angry mouse-eating cats?" Liten guesses.

"No! No! No!" Safari Chip points to Undertaker, Kane, and Liten. "They're better than us because they believe they are."

"That's bogus!" Sammie yells.

Sammie's outburst angers Rodman. "It isn't bogus!" he shoots back.

All heads turn to Rodman. Everyone, including Safari Chip, looks to their new captain to see how he handles confrontation.

"This can be a really great team if we started playing the way I know we can." Rodman turns to Liten. "Liten, you used to be an all-star in Germany I'm told. I know you're afraid of the other teams' cats..."

"And snakes, birds, iguanas, and lizards," Liten interrupts.

"Ok, so there are lots of animals bigger and tougher than you out there. Trust me when I say that no one is going to try to eat you. They might look like they're going to, but it's just to intimidate you."

"He's right," says Safari Chip.

"And if you do get scared, just remember that Undertaker and Kane are out there to protect you," Rodman continues.

"When they're out there," Liten says sarcastically.

Rodman turns to the dogs. "That's right guys. You were brought to here to protect Liten, and you do a great job of that when you're out there. But, let's face it. You're not out there very much, and when you're not out there, not only is Liten unprotected, but we're at an odd man disadvantage."

"We were lucky to only lose by nine," Safari Chip adds.

"But what about hitting them?" Kane asks.

"Other teams hit us all the time. Why don't they get penalized?" Undertaker adds.

"You can hit the other team, but you have to hit them cleanly. You can't blast them so hard that they fly ten feet across the ice, or sneak up behind them, or use your stick," Rodman informs the dogs.

"You guys don't have to tell me what I did wrong." Harlan sits with his head hung low and his flippers held to his cheeks.

"At least you recognize it. Were you trying to stay out of your shell?" Rodman asks.

"I was trying, but I'm still scared."

Safari Chip puts his arm around Harlan. "It's ok Harlan. We'll turn you into a mean, green, puck stopping machine yet."

"So what do you guys say? A little more practice?" Rodman asks.

"Ha!" Sammie interrupts again, and all attention goes back to him. "You talk about teamwork and helping everyone, but what kind of teammate are you? You notice everyone else's flaws, but you didn't once talk about any of your own. Are you perfect?"

"No." Rodman is caught off guard.

Sammie jumps off his table and approaches Rodman menacingly. "And tell me something else. What kind of teammate tattletales on his fellow teammates?" Sammie pokes Rodman in the chest.

Rodman doesn't respond to Sammie's assault, and Sammie storms out of the locker room, leaving an uncomfortable silence. This is not what Rodman had envisioned for his big debut.

Safari Chip walks over to Rodman. "Don't worry about him. He's upset because of his suspension. And to the rest of you guys, I don't usually call out my players, but Sammie's wrong. If he hadn't broken team rules, he wouldn't have gotten in trouble in the first place. So what do you guys say? Will you give Rodman's plan a shot?"

There's an uproarious agreement and a round of high fives. Right away, the mood in the locker room lightens. All of his teammates pat Rodman on the back to let him know they're behind him.

"Ok everyone get in here." Safari Chip rallies the team around in a circle. They put their flippers, hands, wings, paws, and hooves into the center.

"One! Two! Three! Gamblers!"

*

In the Gold Rush locker room, Metz gets his head bandaged. Next to him sits Packer with his head already bandaged. Jason limps around the room past other players with bruises, bandages, and even crutches.

"Do they always play that rough?" Jason complains.

"Yes," answers Packer with a painful grimace.

"How many times do we play them?"

"Twelve times a season. We always win though," Metz puts a positive spin on their beating.

"Oh my gosh! I don't think I'll make it through all twelve games alive," Jason says.

"You probably won't," Packer tells him.

"What!?"

"You probably won't. They average about four season ending injuries to us per season. We only have nine players on the team, so you have a forty-four percent chance of being injured."

"That's insane!" Jason cries with fear filled eyes. Then, suddenly his eyebrows furrow and he smiles his devilish smile. "But if that's how they want to play, we're just going to have to start playing a little rougher."

Chapter 7: Practice And A Whole Lot Of Fun

Rodman exits the elevator and enters the hallway to his hotel room.

Behind Rodman, Ed pokes his head out. "Don't worry about tonight's game Mr. Penguin. That was a tough team to start with. They won't all be that hard."

Rodman smiles. "Thanks Ed."

"We've got faith in you Mr. Rodman sir."

Rodman continues to smile, embarrassed by all the fanfare especially considering the Gamblers got their butts whooped. He digs his key out of his pockets, jams it into the slot, and is about to open his door when the door next to his opens.

Sammie, decked out in a white suit with a black shirt and white tie, steps out and locks eyes with Rodman. "Are you going to tattle on me again?"

"Are you going out past curfew again?" Rodman asks.

"I figure since I don't have a game for a few days, I don't need to worry about some silly curfew."

"I won't have to tell on you. Your appearance when you come into the locker room will give you away."

Sammie grunts and pushes past Rodman.

"Why are you doing this?" Rodman asks. "I hear you used to be an all-star in Fort, Collins, Fresno, and Albuquerque."

Sammie stops. "I was. But do you know what there is to do in those cities?"

"No."

"There's absolutely nothing to do in those cities. But this is Las Vegas. The entertainment capital of the world! There's *so much* to do here. I just can't think about hockey all the time."

It's clear that Sammie has no intention of being a hockey player anymore, and it makes Rodman sad. "Don't you care that you're hurting the team?"

"This team stinks. You saw them play today. Do you really think you can turn them around?" Sammie turns and walks away.

"You should resign from the team then. Someone who can help them deserves your spot."

Sammie ignores Rodman and rounds the corner at the end of the hallway.

*

The Gamblers hold a practice the day after the Gold Rush game. Safari Chip has Harlan work on staying out of his shell while the other players, minus Undertaker and Kane, work on one-timer drills. Near the boards, at center ice, Rodman stands with Undertaker, Kane, and a dummy made up to look like a Gold Rush player.

"So this is illegal." Rodman throws an elbow into the dummy's face, sending the head rocking back and forth rapidly.

Undertaker and Kane laugh so hard they make Rodman chuckle.

"I know it's funny, but it's illegal, and you'll get sent to the penalty box for it. This is also illegal." Rodman skates away from the dummy, stops, and turns around. He skates back as fast as he can with his stick in front of him. He spears the stick completely through the stomach of the dummy.

Undertaker and Kane laugh hysterically. Rodman tries to stop from joining them but he can't. The lifeless Gold Rush dummy with a stick through his tummy is too funny.

"That's called spearing, and as you can see, it can really hurt someone," Rodman says through fits of laughter.

"Yeah. We don't want to kill anyone," says Kane.

"Yeah," Undertaker agrees.

"Good. Because all of these moves are illegal too." Rodman demonstrates cross checking, slashing, hooking, kicking, tripping, boarding, roughing, fighting, and interfering.

Undertaker and Kane crack up while Rodman commits all the penalties on the dummy.

As the dogs' chuckles subside, Rodman asks, "Do you guys get it now?"

"Kind of." Undertaker looks perplexed. "What we don't understand is…"

"What exactly can we do?" Kane finishes

"You can hit the players on the other teams. You just have to do it the right way. For example, grab a puck and pretend to skate towards Harlan," Rodman says to Undertaker.

Undertaker does as he's instructed.

Rodman skates at Undertaker and gently knocks him against the glass. "You have to come in and smash a guy from an angle in which he isn't blindsided by you. And you can smash him as hard as you want as long as you don't come off the ice with your skates. And, don't smash him head first either."

"Oh!" both dogs say.

"You can try this too. Skate at me Kane."

Kane skates at Rodman and is gently knocked to the ice by a shoulder to the chest.

"You can come right at a guy as long as he has the puck or has just passed it as were moving in to smash him."

"That makes sense," says Kane.

"You guys practice these clean hits for a while. I'm going to go check on Harlan." Rodman skates away.

"Sure thing Mr. Penguin," Kane says.

"You got it Hott Rod," Undertaker says.

Rodman takes a spot next to Safari Chip who presides over the shooting and blocking drill. Rodman watches each player take one last shot at Harlan, who still ducks into his shell.

"How's he doing Coach?" Rodman asks.

"CHIP! Chip! Chip! Chip!" Safari Chip hops up and down on the ice.

"Oops! Sorry Coa... Chip. How's he doing?"

"Not very well I'm afraid."

Rodman puts his flipper to his beak, and his eyes move upwards as he thinks. "Hmmm?" An idea comes to him, and he skates to Harlan, who sits on the ice sweating up a storm. "Hi Harlan."

"Hi Rodman," Harlan says with shame in his voice.

"What's the matter my friend?"

"To be honest, I'm still just really scared of the puck."

"I have an idea. And I think it will help Liten with his problem too."

Liten's eyes go wide.

"What have you got in mind?" Safari Chip asks.

"Well..." Rodman starts.

*

Safari Chip, dressed like a drill sergeant, but still wearing his safari hat, marches in front of his players. Most of the Gamblers are dressed in army fatigues, a chest protector, and plastic goggles, and they all hold a paintball gun to their chest. Undertaker and Kane wear fatigues too, but they refuse any protective equipment.

Safari Chip reaches the end of the line of players, does an about-face, marches back the other way, and shouts, "Ok men. We are here to show Harlan T. Turtle that there are many things scarier than getting hit with a puck."

"But paintball isn't scary. It's fun. Back in the old days Undertaker and I..." Kane interrupts his coach until a blue paintball hits him right between the eyes. The gooey paint drips down his forehead all the way to his black nose. "Ouch!"

Safari Chip stands a few yards away, bent in a shooting position, with his gun aimed at Kane. Blue smoke comes from the barrel. He stands up briskly, charges at Kane, and gets right in his face.

Kane leans backwards to get away from the irate monkey.

"Are you scared now Private Fluff Ball?" Safari Chip screams.

"Sir, I am, sir." Kane stands up straight with his chest puffed out.

Safari Chip backs off, giving Kane the opportunity to stand up straight. "Well thank you very much! Now can I be in charge for a while?"

"Sir, you can sir," Kane barks.

"I can't hear you!" Safari Chips hollers.

"Sir, yes sir!" Kane screams.

Safari Chip leaves Kane's side and moves back down the line. "Now!" he yells getting the attention of everyone. "Let me see your war faces."

Kane and Undertaker scrunch their snouts and rear back their lips to show their teeth. Lovey narrows his eyes and tries to roar like a mean grizzly bear, but his teddy bear looks prevent him from looking too mean. He just looks crazy instead. Liten scrunches up his nose and shows his little teeth. Harlan's eyes go round and round in circles, and he snaps his snout. Goose sqwuaks, flickering his tongue as he does and flaps his wings. Maverick nays wildly and whips his head around, making his mane fly all over the place. Rodman tries to make an angry face, but the crazy looks on the faces of all his wild teammates cause him to smile crazily and laugh as the rest of the players scream at the top of their lungs.

"Attack!" Safari Chip fires his paintball gun repeatedly in the air.

The Gamblers jump to life. They run away from each other, shooting at each other as they retreat.

Harlan hides behind the first hiding spot he can find, a stack of hay. Other hiding spaces throughout the field include trees, empty car frames, large metal trash cans, and a small building with a sign out front that reads SAFE HOUSE.

Undertaker and Kane stand in the middle of the field shooting each other at point blank range. Neither flinches as the flesh beneath their fur is pelted with paintballs. Both dogs laugh hysterically as Kane gets covered in the black paint used by Undertaker and Undertaker is covered in the red paint used by Kane.

Maverick and Goose team up and hide behind some trees at the edge of the woods. There, they spot Liten walking just outside the trees. Maverick ventures cautiously out to sneak attack Liten while Goose acts as his wingman, covering him from behind. Despite his efforts to be quiet, Maverick steps on a twig and makes a ruckus loud enough to draw Liten's attention.

Liten whips around and fires erratically in Maverick's direction. He lands a few blind shots on the horse, and Maverick stumbles and falls.

Instinctively, as his brain's self preservation mechanisms kick in, Liten runs towards the noise, firing his paintballs blindly and chaotically. Just like in hockey, he feels the best defense is a strong offense. He fires his gun until he runs out of ammo. At that point, he hides behind a tree and pulls some more paint balls out of his ammo pack to reload. With his gun reloaded, he waits quietly, listening for any sounds of imminent danger. He hears nothing for a long time, so he peeks around the tree to see what he can see. Immediately, he's met by a shot of yellow paint on one of his giant ears. The sting and the shock take him by surprise, but he quickly recovers and sees Goose running at him with Maverick, smattered with Liten's grey paint, right behind him. The mouse turns tail and runs away from the crazy-eyed fowl and revenge seeking horse.

Rodman pokes his head out from behind a car frame. Empty field is all he sees. He steps out from behind the frame and ventures a few feet into the open field to get a better look. The entire field is seemingly empty. He throws his flippers to his side and lets out a heavy sigh. Before the sigh completely escapes his mouth, a purple paintball hits him in the shoulder. The surprise of the shot and the mini punch that comes with it cause him to drop his gun.

Lovey runs at Rodman, firing with reckless abandon.

Rodman reaches feverishly for his paintball gun. Each second he's unable to grab ahold of it, a barrage of purple paint rains down on him. Finally, he retrieves his gun, but he sees he has no chance at gaining the upper hand, so he runs away from Lovey's attack, laughing all the while.

Lovey chases Rodman across the open field, peppering his buddy with paint. Neither sees Safari Chip lined up to their side. Nor do they see that he's traded his paintball gun for a paintball bazooka. They run unwittingly into the line of fire, and Safari Chip fires a blast heard all over the field.

Lovey gets hit with a giant blast of blue paint that splatters his entire side and takes him six inches off the ground and six feet through the air.

Intuitively, Rodman falls to the ground at the sound. Once he realizes he's unharmed, he notices he's no longer being hit by Lovey's fire. He turns his head to check on the teddy bear and sees him lying on the ground unmoving and drenched in paint. Rodman looks around but doesn't see who did this to Lovey. He can't tell where the shot came from, but gets up and runs to check on Lovey anyway. "Are you ok Lovey?"

Lovey's eyes are closed, and he says nothing.

"Lovey?" Rodman asks.

No response from the teddy bear.

"Lovey?" Rodman shakes his friend.

Lovey's eyes open. "Did I step on a paintball landmine or something?"

"Nope," Safari Chip calls as he walks triumphantly up to them holding his bazooka in the air. "I got you with this."

"Wicked," Lovey smiles.

"That's pretty neat Coach," Rodman says.

Safari Chip furrows his brow and points the bazooka at him.

"I mean Chip," Rodman quickly corrects himself.

Safari Chip perks up. "Yeah, it's really cool, but the downside is that it only has the capacity to hold one shot."

The wheels in Rodman's head turn. "One shot?"

"Yeah," Safari Chip answers.

Rodman aims his gun at his coach. Safari Chip freaks out and turns to run away. He doesn't get far before Rodman starts spraying him with white paint.

Lovey, as he's left alone, takes the opportunity to get up and run away. He runs to the bale of hay where Harlan hides. He scares the turtle, causing Harlan to fumble his gun as he tries to raise it in self defense. Lovey takes a seat next to the nervous turtle, and Harlan can see he's not in attack mode, so he calms down.

"Hey Harlan," the half cream colored half blue paint splattered bear greets him.

"Hi Lovey. What happened to you?"

"Chip hit me with a paint ball bazooka."

"Does it hurt?"

"Not really," Lovey answers. "Haven't you been shot yet?"

"I've been hiding. I always seem..." Harlan begins but he's interrupted by a point blank blast from Lovey. Purple paint splatters all over his flipper and his eyes go wide. "Ouch!"

"Not too bad right?" Lovey asks.

"I'd rather get hit with a puck. At least then I have padding on."

"Well, you better get out there and start paintballing, or I'm going to do it again." Lovey waves his gun at Harlan.

Harlan stands up and runs from behind the hay for his life. He turns and sees Lovey standing up aim to shoot more paint, so Harlan fires a green shot at him as he runs away.

Instead of firing back at Harlan, Lovey calls to the other Gamblers, who are too busy shooting each other to notice Harlan. "Hey!"

Everyone turns their attention to Lovey.

He points to Harlan. "There goes Harlan."

Harlan sees nine different sets of eyes lock onto him. He knows his only chance is to make a break for the safe house about thirty yards away. He runs as fast as his little green legs will carry him. Meanwhile, the other Gamblers stop shooting each other and chase him like greyhounds to a mechanical bunny.

Harlan, cursed with being one of the slowest animals of all time, and by far the slowest on the team, sweats and pants as he runs to the safe house. For a short time, he's able to dodge his teammate's paintballs. They fly past and around him, but as the other Gamblers close in, their shots grow more accurate. His shell, legs, and flippers get drilled with different colored paint.

Despite his lack of speed, he makes it to the front door of the safe house before the others can catch him. He reaches for the handle, turns it, and finds it's locked. Panic washes over him. There's nowhere left to run. He throws down his gun and raises a leg to his chest and his flippers to his face in a vain attempt to protect himself from the onslaught of animals racing at him with paintball guns aimed and paintballs flying at him. As the other Gamblers reach him, Harlan slinks to the ground, closes his eyes, and covers up as much of his body as he can. He waits for a while expecting to get absolutely hammered, but to his surprise, he doesn't feel any anything, so he peeks out from behind his flippers. He sees his teammates and his coach encircled around and over him. They have their guns aimed, and shoot only once they see him looking at them. They shoot Harlan up with a rainbow of paintballs until he's completely covered. When he feels that it's neither painful nor scary, he opens up, no longer protecting himself from the blasts, taking on their shots. He reaches for his gun and fires back.

Soon, everyone is taking shots at everyone else.

After paintball, the Gamblers return their guns and other equipment. All are in high spirits and still covered in paint when they pile back into their limo.

Harlan stops Rodman and Safari Chip before they get in. "I just want to say thanks. I think this experience is really going to help me in the net."

"That's good," says Rodman with a sly grin. "But we're not done."

"That's right. We're not done." Safari Chip matches Rodman's grin.

"There's more?" Harlan asks nervously.

"We've only just begun!" Safari Chip informs him.

*

The Gamblers, wearing swimming trunks and t-shirts, exit their limo outside the Golden Chunk Hotel downtown. They make their way to the hotel's pool area. Once there, no one notices anything particularly scary, but as they give the pool a closer look, there are many nervous gasps.

Harlan is near the back of the crowd and can't see over the much taller Undertaker and Kane. He pushes his way to the front of the group where revealed to him is a massive swimming pool with a giant fish tank positioned right in the center. Its walls reach the ceiling above, thus keeping the contents of the tank separate from the pool. Instead of fish inside the tank though, there are sharks and a transparent waterslide that passes through.

Rodman and Safari Chip smile devilishly at the mortified looks of the others. Suddenly, no one wants to go swimming.

"Come on boys." Safari Chips motions for the team to follow.

No one budges, and Rodman has to herd them along like cattle. He pushes them along to a set of stairs that lead up to the slide. Before going up, he makes sure everyone else has gone ahead of him.

Harlan eyeballs the ravenous sharks through the glass walls of the tank as he ascends the stairs. They seem to be eyeballing him back. Harlan's scared, but he isn't the only one terrified of the shark infested slide. Even the team's designated tough guys, Undertaker and Kane, are hesitant to take this plunge.

Atop the slide, Safari Chip motions for Harlan to come to the front of the line.

"I'm ok back here Chip. I'll watch the others go down first." Harlan stands pat.

"Get up here Turtle," Safari Chip demands.

Harlan gulps, cringes, and moves slowly to the front of the line.

Undertaker hums Chopin's *Funeral March.*

"Shut up Undertaker," Harlan says as he passes the dog.

"Go ahead and sit down," Safari Chip orders Harlan.

Harlan hesitates again. He looks down the slide warily. It's dark and covered at first. He wonders how long it lasts before it spits its riders into a brightly lit and transparent slide, illuminating them to the sharks. He looks back to his coach. "I don't think I want to. I'm not scared of the puck anymore. After paintball, I know I can stand up to shots on goal."

Safari Chip sighs and shrugs. "Fine. I guess I can't *make* you go."

Harlan is relieved. At the end of the line, Rodman looks perplexed. He thought they were going to show Harlan what it is to be *really* scared.

Harlan starts to walk away, but Safari Chip steps in his path. They collide, and Safari Chip's hat flies off of his head and lands on the slide's platform. The rushing waters push the hat towards the slope at the entrance of the slide.

"My hat!" Safari Chip shouts.

"Don't worry. I'll get it!" Harlan turns, bends over, reaches for the hat, and grasps it firmly. "I got it."

From behind, Safari Chip gives Harlan a light kick in the pants, sending him falling head first down the slide to the excited cheers and screams of the rest of the Gamblers.

Harlan goes to pieces inside the dark tunnel, screaming at the top of his lungs and clutching Safari Chip's hat for dear life. He unexpectedly rounds a darkened corner and is shot into the lighted part of the tunnel. Though he finds himself still safely tucked inside the protective walls of the slide, the walls themselves seem to disappear. A light brown shark with dark brown spots lunges at him and hits the side of the slide. Harlan clutches his heart and nearly faints, but he's able to keep his eyes open and remain conscious. Another shark, a grey one that looks like a smaller great white, takes a shot at him from the other side, and he screams again. The second attempt on his life is just as scary, but he realizes he's safe. By the third time a shark tries to strike him, he's almost totally relaxed. As he slides further and further, he actually begins to enjoy the ride. He even starts making faces at the sharks. Before he knows it, the ride is over, and he's spit into the pool with a splash.

Atop the slide, the rest of the Gamblers argue about who's to go next. Lovey plays rock paper scissors with Undertaker and Kane at the same time for who gets to go last. Maverick and Goose try to push each other closer to the front of the line. Liten pleads with Rodman and Safari Chip to be excused from this adventure.

Everyone breathes a sigh of relief when they see Harlan running safely back up the stairs wearing Safari Chip's hat. He rushes towards them with his flippers flailing excitedly about. They try to question him about the slide, but he hurries past them too excited to go again to answer all their questions. He flies by and dives head first down the slide yelling, "This is so fun."

No one can believe it. Did he really just say this was fun?

The fight for who gets to go last turns into a fight for who gets to go next. All the Gamblers make a mad dash for the platform. Liten reaches the platform first, but he's pulled back and pushed aside by Undertaker and Kane. Maverick and Goose push past the mouse too, only to fight each other at the slide entrance. Maverick wins the fight and goes first, but Goose follows quickly behind. Liten is pushed aside again, this time by Lovey and Rodman. The angry mouse waves a fist at the back of their heads and then, with no one left to push him around, he jumps down too. Safari Chip waits for all his players to go before he too jumps into the slide.

The Gamblers slip, slide, twist, and splash down the slide, watching, pointing, and making silly faces at the sharks as they go. After they're shot into the pool, they swim to the enormous walls of the tank and admire the oceanic beasts.

They continue to ride the slide, swim, play, and do some team bonding for a couple of hours.

Afterwards, in normal clothes, they head out of the Golden Chunk to their limo. It takes them to a 1,500 foot tall hotel called the Atmosphere. From the outside, the Gamblers stare up at the hotel's astounding stature. Safari Chip lets his players take a gander and then leads them inside where they make their way to an elevator that leads to the viewing deck at the top.

Once they get all the way to the top, Safari Chip doesn't allow them to look out at the view. He wants that to be a surprise, so instead, he directs them to a line for a ride located over a quarter mile off the ground. The rollercoaster-like ride has carts set on tracks, but instead of going round and round, it goes straight into the air on a very small set of tracks. It appears the carts are poised to be shot right into space once it reaches the end of the tracks, but the Gamblers know that cannot be the case. They all gulp at the terrifying ride and wonder what sort of mess they've gotten into. When the time comes for them to enter the carts, they race for the seats in the back of the ride. Liten and Safari Chip get the very back. Maverick and Goose get the seats just in front of them. Lovey sits in a seat by himself in the middle row. Undertaker and Kane want to sit close and take the seats just behind the front row, but the front row is reserved for Rodman and Harlan.

Everyone gets strapped in, and the ride begins to move. There's a mixture of fear and excitement all around. The carts start climbing up the tracks, and Harlan closes his eyes, but Rodman reaches over and pries them open. He gives Harlan a reassuring wink and a thumbs up. Harlan smiles nervously and keeps his eyes open.

The ride moves upwards and stops at a very steep angle half way up the track. The Gamblers remain deathly quiet and still for what seems like forever.

"What's going on?" Lovey asks.

"Yes. Is it broken?" Liten asks.

"Boy I hope so," Harlan says. He tries to look over his shoulder to see the ground, but suddenly the ride moves up the tracks a bit more and the tracks tip, sending all the Gamblers hurdling over the building's edge with reckless abandon towards the streets of the Las Vegas Strip.

Screams go around as they fall, and their hands inadvertently fly up. Just when it seems they're going to plummet to certain doom, the ride locks up and they stop. Their screams turn to sighs of relief and slight laughter. Slowly, the ride starts pulling them back. They continue to laugh until the ride drops again without warning and they all start screaming like little girls once more. After the second fall, they're left to dangle over the side for a few moments. Most of them take in the site of the town and all its lights that has come into full and perfect view.

Undertaker and Kane spit over the edge and try unsuccessfully to follow the drops to the ground.

Harlan, with each new adventure, feels more and more confident about being able to stand pat in goal.

The ride does a few more pulls and drops and then pulls them back up for good. They exit the ride and rush to the viewing platform. Rodman admires the glow from the hotel lights and how they blur into the nighttime sky. They remain atop the Atmosphere, getting dinner and taking in the view before jumping back into their limo.

They take a short ride to a beat up old hotel called The Greek. Parked in front of the hotel is a small black and white bus with the words LAS VEGAS GHOST TOURS on its side. The Gamblers trade their limo for the bus. Excited whispers and laughs swirl around the bus. No one except Safari Chip can sit still. Speculation abounds about what sort of ghosts they'll see.

The bus driver and tour guide, a raven named Mr. Price, is dressed in a crooked black top hat, a mortician-like tuxedo, and a black and red cape. The first stop the bus makes is at the Pink Penguin hotel.

Mr. Price leads the team through the hotel to the pool area beyond a maze of foliage, shrubberies, waterfalls, and miniature buildings. He takes them through one of the buildings, a museum with artifacts from the hotel's founder, Bugsy Seagull. As they look around, Mr. Price recounts the legend of Bugsy Seagull and the Pink Penguin.

"Bugsy was a gangster throughout the 1930's and part of the 1940's. He made a fortune stealing from gangsters. And with that fortune he built the Pink Flamingo. He named it after his girlfriend, a penguin who always wore pink. He grew to love the hotel so much that he established permanent residence here. In fact, some say he's still here.

"To the FBI, Bugsy was no better than the gangsters he stole from. They were always trying to get dirt on him so they could put him in jail, but somehow or another he always avoiding doing time. The feds weren't Bugsy's only enemies though. His long list of enemies included gangsters, investors of the Pink Penguin who felt they had been cheated out of the profits, and plenty of other animals he rubbed the wrong way.

"One of those animals was Quackey Donaldson. Aside from being a gangster who had been swindled by Bugsy, one night Bugsy smashed his car into Quackey's brand new 1941 Cadillac. When the police came, Bugsy threw a couple of dollars their way and talked his way out of the ticket and the responsibility of paying for the damage to Quackey's car. Quackey swore revenge.

"Two years later, on November 16th, 1943, Bugsy didn't show up to his daily board meeting at the Pink Penguin. The board sent a porter to check on Bugsy and found his room empty. All his stuff was still there, his hat, his watch, his wallet. But Bugsy was gone and was never seen again. To this day, no one knows what happened to him. One theory is that on the night of his disappearance, all of his enemies got together and exterminated him. Another theory is that he fled the country because he knew the FBI was about to swoop in and get him. Other's think that the members of the board at the Pink Penguin had him rubbed out in an effort to gain control of the hotel.

"No matter what happened to him, one thing is for sure. If he's alive today, it's only in spirit. Some say they've seen his ghostly presence here in the museum and around the maze of trees and shrubs outside. They say he wanders around looking for the fun and excitement that was always around during the opening days of the hotel."

The Gamblers all look around to see if they can catch a glimpse of Bugsy.

Mr. Price leads the Gamblers to a plaque dedicated to Bugsy just outside the museum as he finishes the story of the vanished bird. "It's here, just outside his former residence, where Bugsy is most often seen. Feel free to take a few pictures. Perhaps you'll capture the former hotel owner in one."

The Gamblers each throw Mr. Price a camera and run to pose in front of the plaque. Mr. Price seems faintly annoyed that he has to take nine photos, but he performs the task for the paying customers. After the final photo is taken, the Gamblers run to the pile of cameras and sort through them to find their own. They feverishly go to their photo menu and check for a glimpse of a ghost. To their dismay, none of their pictures seem to have anything out of the ordinary in them.

Then, Lovey shouts, "Wait! I think I see something in mine."

Everyone, including Mr. Price, huddles around Lovey and looks into his picture viewer.

"Where?" Maverick asks.

"I don't see anything," Kane says.

"Me neither," agrees Undertaker.

"Right there." Lovey points to a grayish, silvery blob in the picture.

Everyone looks closer at the object.

"I still don't see anything," Rodman says.

"Oh for Heaven's sakes right there. You can see a face, torso, arms, and legs right there," says an unfamiliar voice. A smoky grey, almost transparent, wing reaches in and points at the photo.

At first, everyone examines the photo where the feathers attached to the mystery wing points. A seagull dressed in a three piece suit and a fedora floating in the background is faintly visible. They all oooh and ahhh at the spooky sight.

"That's creepy," Harlan says.

"Yeah, but it's cool," Lovey says.

"Thanks for pointing it out Goose," Maverick says.

"I didn't point it out," Goose says.

"You didn't?" Maverick asks.

"No."

"Then whose wing was that?" Rodman asks.

At the same time, the Gamblers and Mr. Price turn in the direction from which the wing came from. There before them floats the smiling carefree spirit of Bugsy Seagull.

Shrieks of fear ring out from the Gamblers and their guide. They can't run fast enough away from the haunted hotel. They fly by patrons and workers who look on disturbed at the animals freaking out and causing a scene.

Back on the bus, everyone takes a seat and Mr. Price puts the pedal to the metal. He yells to the Gamblers from the driver's wheel. "Folks we do apologize for that. Las Vegas Ghost Tours is purely an entertainment driven company and cannot be held liable for any ghosts, ghouls, or specters that might visit us tonight." He pauses for a few seconds. "And to be honest, that sort of thing has never happened before, so if anyone wants to quit now, just let me know, and a full refund of your money will be promptly given."

The Gamblers look around at each other shaken, but their nervous looks rapidly change to excited grins and cheers. They insist on continuing. As scary as it was seeing a ghost, they're safe now and have their fingers crossed they run into more.

Mr. Price takes them to a park haunted by the spirit of a dog who got run over and is claimed to be seen chasing cars at night. He also takes them to a giant translucent business tower that was the scene of an accident in which a bird flew right into a window high upon the thirty-fifth floor, suffering mortal injuries. There, he's supposedly seen flying in one spot against the building as if he can't see it or move past it. Their fourth destination is a boarded up abandon house where one of the construction workers, a woodpecker, got trapped inside while he napped on the job. He tried pecking his way out but never made it. Neighbors say pecking can be heard all night until the sun comes up.

The second to last stop on the tour is the former residence of legendary Las Vegas comedian J.E. Sanford, a red fox, whom is said to haunt the place. Sanford bought the house with his first big paycheck as an entertainer and lived there until his death of natural causes. The home was sold to a real estate agent and transformed into an office. The agent would later make claims that Sanford, though dead, never left the house. He said that strange things began to happen when he moved in. The letters on his computer screen would change from black to red when no one was looking, loud pool parties could be heard in the parking lot that used to be the elegant backyard with a giant pool, and the apparition of J.E. Sanford himself would scare clients away. The agent was going to sell the building, but one day he honored the comedian with an insignia of a red fox on the bottom of the sign out front. Since then, the spirit has been quieter but will occasionally come out if provoked.

Rodman is particularly impressed by the story of J.E. Sanford. He wonders if he'll one day be considered a Las Vegas icon like Sanford and Seagull. He sure hopes so.

After the home of J.E. Sanford, Mr. Price drives to what he calls the most haunted spot of any town, the main cemetery. The cemetery is dark, wide open, and flat out scary. Everyone gets off the bus and sticks close together, except Undertaker and Kane, who run out ahead into the graveyard. The rest of the team walks cautiously behind Mr. Price as he tells them all sorts of ghost stories.

Harlan bites the tip of his flipper as he walks. He looks around guardedly and tries to keep up, but deep into the cemetery, he finds himself falling behind because Liten keeps calling for him to wait up.

The mouse is just as scared and watchful as Harlan. He turns around at every little noise to make sure everything is ok. He calls again for to Harlan to wait up.

Harlan stops and waits.

"This is seriously creepy and twisted," Liten complains as he catches up to the turtle.

"I agree," Harlan says.

"I do not want any more to do with this part of the tour. I am going back to the bus. You should come with me." Liten hopes to have company on the walk back.

"Trust me. I want to go back to the bus as bad as you, but this whole trip is meant to help me overcome my fears. I'd feel bad if I backed out now."

"You are a true warrior Harlan. Stay brave." Liten turns and makes the trek back.

Harlan continues on, passing many tombstones. He can't see or hear the rest of the team ahead of him in the dark. He knows the path only leads in one direction though, so they must be there. He hurries along and thinks he hears voices and eerie creaking as he moves further down the path.

Behind Harlan, Liten runs into the same thing. His mind tricks him into thinking he's hearing voices coming from the graves and the creaking of coffins opening. He moves a little quicker and steps on the metallic curved point of a shovel that has been left on the path. The stick end of the shovel comes up and almost hits him in the face. He squeals in terror and turns to run back to Harlan.

Harlan hears the squeals but doesn't know what they are, and he doesn't care to find out either. He runs full sprint away until he comes upon two colossal tombstones. Just as he runs alongside the first tombstone, Undertaker jumps from behind it, barking like a rabid dog. Harlan almost leaps out of his shell. He turns away from Undertaker and faces the other mammoth tombstone only to have Kane jump from behind that one, barking as well. Harlan shrieks and falls down on his tail. He tries to catch his breath and regain his normal heartbeat as the dogs laugh hysterically at him. A feeling of relief washes over Harlan when he realizes he's safe, and he joins the dogs in their laughter.

They hear Liten's screams growing closer. "Harlan! Help me! There are ghosts trying to get me!"

Harlan whispers to the dogs. "Let's get Liten."

Undertaker and Kane grin from ear to ear. They suppress their laughter, and all three hide behind one of the tombstones. They wait with flippers and paws over their mouths to conceal their laughter. The excitement of knowing that they're about to scare the pants off of Liten is almost too much to bear. Harlan has to restrain the dogs from jumping out too early.

Liten comes into view. He runs, exhausted and out of breath, towards the tombstone. Harlan and the dogs let him pass before they jump out screaming at him. Liten falls down, shields his face with his paws, and lets out the girliest of screams.

Harlan and the dogs laugh uncontrollably.

Liten cracks his fingers enough to let one of his eyes peek out. He sees the brutes Undertaker and Kane joined by Harlan laughing at him. "You think that was funny do you?"

"Well it wasn't *not* funny," Kane laughs.

Liten picks himself off the ground. His whole body shakes and his arms flail as he shouts at them, "You are lucky I am not a fighter!"

The trio continues laughing at him as he stomps off.

Then, in the middle of their laughter, from behind them, a skeleton hand taps Harlan on the shoulder. "Guys!" Harlan calls to the dogs and points to the tapping bones.

Undertaker and Kane see the bones, and all three turn around to see a skeleton waving at them. They scream and run away even quicker than Liten. Once they're out of sight, the skeleton reaches up and pulls off his mask to reveal a very amused Rodman.

*

On the bus back to The Greek, Rodman sits next to Safari Chip.

"I have to admit Rodman. I really think all this scary stuff has helped Harlan. Only time will tell, but if he can handle paintballs, sharks, ghosts, graveyards, and rollercoasters, then I think getting in the way of a puck won't be a problem for him. But, I thought you said this scary stuff might help Liten too."

Rodman smiles triumphantly. "Oh yeah. We have one more stop."

*

The Gamblers limo pulls up outside the MRM Hotel. They're dropped off at the front doors of the aqua green hotel with over five thousand rooms. Above the entrance is a bronze statue of a lion that stands eighty feet high. Safari Chip takes one look at the hotel and immediately knows what Rodman is up to.

The rest of the team has no clue what's going on here, but they're excited to find out. The MRM is much larger than the New Orleans Hotel, and the place has a totally different feel on the inside. Whereas the New Orleans Hotel is extremely bright with red and gold lighting everywhere, the lighting in the MRM's casino is dark with a subtle cool blue ambiance that comes from a much higher ceiling.

Right smack dab in the middle of the casino is a lion habitat behind large glass windows. The giant cats walk around, growling and acting ferocious for the gathered crowd. Even the Gamblers stop to gawk. Liten shudders at the sight.

"Come on guys." Rodman keeps them moving to a door next to the lion habitat. He flashes a pass of some sort to the guard and they're allowed to enter. Rodman leads the team to another door. This one is unguarded and unlocked. He motions for the team to enter the pitch black room.

Liten and Harlan walk in first. Once they're inside, Rodman slams the door shut. The mouse and turtle have no way out. Panic sets into both. They can't see a thing, and even trying to find a light switch is a chore.

"Hey! What's going on?" Harlan asks.

"Let us out. What goes on here?" Liten yells.

Together, they pound on the door and demand to be let out. Liten continues to fumble around for a light switch but can't find one. Harlan pounds harder and yells louder. Still, nothing comes from the other side of the door. Behind them, another door opens. They both stop moving.

"What was that?" Liten whispers, his sense of danger kicking into high gear.

Harlan's fright is so much that he can't find the means to speak. They hear a light growl from across the room and shudder uncontrollably. They each feel they'd be safer if only they could turn on a light. As though an answer to their prayers, the lights come on, but both of them immediately wish they were back in the dark when they're met by one of the lions from the habitat. He stands on his hind legs with his mouth wide open, displaying his razor-sharp teeth. He roars ferociously, causing Harlan to faint. Liten turns back to the door and scratches like a madman.

"Let us out! Oh please let us out!" Liten screams.

The lion roars louder. Then his roars turn to a cough and a hack. Liten stops scratching at the door and turns to see the lion coughing and gagging. Finally, the lion hacks up a giant hair ball and discards it in a nearby wastebasket.

"Oh dear. Do please excuse me," the lion says in a very proper British accent. He walks to a changing partition, reaches behind it, and grabs a red robe.

"Wh-Wh-Hello?" Liten's confused. He watches the lion closely for any sudden movements.

"Where are my manners? My name is Alston Leon." The lion bows and makes his way closer to Liten. He extends his massive paw for a friendly handshake. Before Liten can extend his tiny paw, Alston notices the unconscious turtle on the floor. "Oh bother. We better get your friend off the ground." Alston slides one paw under Harlan's shell and another under his head. He helps Harlan sit up under the cautious watch of Liten.

Harlan opens his eyes slowly.

"Hello chap," Alston greets the turtle.

Harlan looks to Liten with panic in his eyes.

"Don't worry. It's ok... I think." Liten says.

"Oh quite, quite," Alston assures them. "I understand the two of you are trying to get over some fears."

Harlan stands on his own accord close to Liten.

Alston pats both on the head and moves back into the furnished lion's den. He motions for the two Gamblers to follow.

The Gamblers look to each other before Liten leads Harlan to a couch in the room.

"You're not going to eat us?" Harlan asks.

"Heavens no! What sort of a world would this be if everyone went around eating everyone else?" Alston chuckles.

"But, I'm a mouse. Cats eat mice," Liten argues a case for nature.

"That's a complete misnomer. Cats don't eat mice. We like fish for the most part. Perhaps a nice salad." Alston plops into a comfy, plush, red, leather chair.

"You seem so angry in your habitat," Harlan notes from the couch across from Alston.

"That's all for show. I've got to give the crowd what they came to see. They don't want to watch The King Of The Jungle sit down and read a book. They want to see me roar. And pounce. And terrorize my chew toys." Alston is animated and loud as he talks. "In all actuality though, I like nothing more than relaxing with a good book." He pulls a copy of *The Grapes of Wrath* from under his chair and holds it up. "This meeting was set up by your friend, Mr. Rodman to show you Mr. Liten that you need not fear cats. After all, I'm the biggest cat in the world, and I'm not going to eat you. We live in a civilized society. We do go around eating one another. And, if I'm not going to eat you, you really don't need to fear a couple of little old house cats on the Gold Rush. And you Mr. Harlan, it was meant to strengthen your view that you need not fear the puck."

"What a relief," Liten sighs.

"No doubt," Harlan agrees.

Alston stands up abruptly and scares Liten and Harlan to their feet. Alston jumps, startled by their sudden movement. All three burst into laughter.

Alston puts his huge arms around Liten and Harlan. "That's not all I've been commissioned to do either. I've also been granted front row season tickets to the remainder of your games, so I can be there as a reminder to you boys that no matter how bad things may be out there, as long as you're with your team, everything will be fine."

"Really?" Liten asks.

"You'd do that for us?" Harlan asks.

"I would, and I shall. Not only do I enjoy reading, but I also enjoy a good sporting contest." Alston double pumps his fists, and walks the Gamblers to the door. "Remember, where ever you see a cat trying to smash you, I'll be there. Whenever you see a puck flying at you, I'll be there."

Harlan and Liten smile and nod at Alston as he opens the door to reveal the rest of the Gamblers outside smiling slyly. The team heads down the hallway away from the lion's den.

Rodman turns to Alston and salutes him appreciatively.

Alston stands up straight and salutes him back.

Chapter 8: The Gamblers vs. The Idaho Potatoes

At the Gamblers next practice, Harlan does very well standing up against shots. Undertaker and Kane demonstrate some disciplined checks against their teammates. Safari Chip even has some old teammates from his playing days, "Jungle" Jim Jones, a panther, and Otto "High Tree" Jones, a mountain cat, come to practice. The Joneses, no relation, practice side by side with Liten, who doesn't think twice about their feline pedigrees. Practice goes well. All are excited to get out and showcase their improvements in a real game.

When their next game arrives, the Gamblers make sure their skates are extra sharp, their sticks extra taped, and their padding extra padded.

Despite their excitement, Safari Chip comes out of his office and finds the locker room full of anxious silence. He opens his mouth to tell his team it's game time, but the silence overwhelms him. He's never seen them act this way. He scratches his head and then yells, "Alright everyone. Game time!"

The Gamblers spring to life, yelling and screaming as they run for the locker room exit with Rodman leading the charge. Safari Chip gets wrapped up in their sudden burst of energy. He just knows they're going to destroy their opponents tonight. He gets so pumped that he runs out of the locker room, into the tunnel, and down the corridor with them.

The Gamblers barge onto the ice like a runaway freight train. They don't even wait for their nightly introductions. Safari Chip runs halfway to the bench before composing himself and appropriately walking the rest of the way.

After the National Anthem, everyone skates by Harlan and taps his pads with their sticks.

Rodman lines up for the game's first faceoff across from the Idaho Potatoes captain, Lance Maulbreath, a thuggish tiger known for his overly assertive and unscrupulous play. If it weren't for Jason, Maulbreath would be the top goon in the league. He's big and intimidating.

As they wait for the puck to be dropped, Maulbreath curls back his upper lip, showing Rodman his knife-like teeth.

Rodman, showing no fear, smiles back at the tiger.

The referee drops the puck, and the two captains fight like dueling cavaliers for it. In the end, Rodman wins and sends the puck to Undertaker. Undertaker takes the puck up the ice and passes it to Lovey.

Lovey dekes around one of the Potatoes defenders, finds an open lane, and shoots the puck at the goalie. The goalie drops to a knee, stretches out his other leg, and blocks the shot. The puck gets kicked back onto the ice and into the continuing play.

Rodman races to get the rebound. He beats Maulbreath by a split second and slaps a shot up and over the goalie's left shoulder. The puck rattles around the back of the net. Goal lights go off. One of the referees indicates goal. The goalie spins around and sees the puck resting behind the goal line.

Rodman throws his flippers up in celebration. Undertaker and Kane almost knock him down as they skate in fast and throw their arms around him in celebration. Lovey comes in from his left and Liten from his right to join the group hug. The celebration is especially exciting because not only are goals rare for them, but goals that give them the lead are almost nonexistent.

The Potatoes watch annoyed as the over-the-top celebration makes its way to the Gamblers bench and is greeted by high fives from Maverick, Goose, and Safari Chip.

"Good job guys. That's our first lead of the season. Keep it going," Safari Chip shouts.

The line of celebrating Gamblers makes its way to Harlan. They each give him a fist pound.

"Keep it up guys. Nothing's getting past me tonight." Harlan tips his stick at them.

With a swagger unmatched, Rodman returns to center ice for another faceoff. He turns his head to the bench and gives his coach and other teammates a thumbs up. The referee drops the puck before Rodman is ready. He loses the faceoff and gets bowled over by Maulbreath. Rodman doesn't stay down for long. He springs to his feet and skates quickly to the play.

Up the ice, Rodman sees Kane racing side by side with a chimpanzee on the Potatoes, Bing Hope. Kane tries to disrupt Bing's handling of the puck. Rodman watches in horror as Kane rides the chimp towards the boards and slams him into the glass. Rodman freezes, anticipating a whistle and a penalty, but when he looks to the referees, they do nothing. Rodman smiles impressed at Kane's good play. He wants to applaud the dog, but he knows he has to finish the play. He turns his attention back to the play and is mortified to see Undertaker fly in, both skates off the ice, and smash Bing illegally into the glass.

Whistles blow all over the ice. Members of both teams skate towards Undertaker and Bing. Pushing, shoving, and angry words go round and round from one team to the other. The referees struggle to separate the teams. It takes over two minutes to get the skirmish broken up. When it's all said and done, the Potatoes trainer and one of their players are needed to help Bing to his feet.

One of the referees makes a boarding signal with his hands. "Boarding. Number thirteen. Las Vegas. Five minutes. Game misconduct. Number thirteen is out of the game." He grabs Undertaker by the arm and leads him off the ice.

Undertaker barks at the referee. "What did I do?"

Rodman skates to Undertaker and muzzles him with his flipper. He takes Undertaker from the referee. "Quiet Undertaker. You're going to make the penalty worse."

Undertaker waits for Rodman to remove his flipper before he argues. "I thought I could hit him if he saw it coming."

"But you came off your feet. You can't do that, and you smashed his head into the glass. You can't do that either."

"Oh shucks Hott Rod. I forgot."

Rodman and Undertaker reach the tunnel. "Did you see how Kane hit the guy?"

"Yeah."

"Notice how he didn't get a whistle and gets to stay to hit more guys?" Rodman appeals to Undertaker's more aggressive side.

Undertaker's eyes light up. "Yeah!"

The doors to the tunnel are opened up by security.

"Next time Undertaker. Next time," Rodman gives Undertaker a thumbs up and races back to the game.

Overhead, the arena announcer broadcasts the penalty to the crowd. Kane serves Undertaker's penalty and is replaced on the ice by Maverick.

A referee summons Rodman and Maulbreath to the area just outside the penalty box. Before the referee can say anything to the captains, Rodman offers an apology on behalf of Undertaker.

"That was a dirty hit Rodman. I don't want to see anymore of that," the referee warns.

"Yeah man. Bing probably has a concussion," Maulbreath bellyaches.

"Seriously guys, Undertaker didn't mean to hurt anyone. We'll get him fixed up good," Rodman promises.

"Fix it quick." The referee skates back to center ice for the next faceoff.

"The ref may have let you guys off with a warning, but I believe in an eye for an eye. I'd watch your mouse if I were you." Maulbreath flashes Rodman his shimmering teeth.

Rodman steps up to Maulbreath threateningly. "You better leave him alone. He didn't do anything."

Maulbreath shoves Rodman, and Rodman shoves him back. Maulbreath puts his paw on Rodman's face and shoves his head. Rodman jumps at the tiger and fisticuffs ensue. Rodman gains the upper hand with a swift punch to Maulbreath's face. The tiger is dazed by the blow, and after a few more hits from Rodman, he falls on his tail.

Whistles blow. It takes Lovey, Maverick, and Liten to restrain Rodman and two referees and two Potatoes players to restrain Maulbreath. The third referee points at Rodman and then Maulbreath. "Penalty! Penalty! Five minutes for fighting."

Rodman joins Kane in the penalty box and Maulbreath enters his alone. They continue to point fingers and jaw through the glass. The crowd eggs them on. Maulbreath stands up and walks to the glass that separates the penalty boxes. He throws his arms up at Rodman, and the irate penguin flies off his bench and slams into the glass, causing Maulbreath to flinch backwards. Rodman tries to climb the glass to get to Maulbreath, but Kane restrains him.

On the Gamblers bench, Safari Chip shakes his head in disbelief and disappointment. The game had gotten off to such a good start, and now his captain is serving a fighting penalty, one defenseman is serving a five minute penalty for another defenseman who's been thrown out of the game, and his team is going to be on the penalty kill for the next five minutes. He questions whether or not this team can be turned around, even with Rodman's help.

Play continues with the Gamblers doing their best to hang in, but less than a minute into the penalty kill, the Potatoes tie the game. Twenty-four seconds after that, they score again. The Gamblers alternate Goose in and out for tired players whenever they can, but it doesn't help much. The fatigued Gamblers are no match for the Potatoes one man advantage.

By the time the penalties are up, the Potatoes score four times. Fresh out of the penalty box, Rodman and Maulbreath race for a loose puck. Rodman wins the race but is checked hard against the glass by an elbow. He falls down and looks towards the nearest referee for a whistle but none is blown.

Liten watches Rodman take the dirty hit. He then sees Alston in the crowd waving an encouraging fist. Liten turns his attention back to Maulbreath and scowls. He mans up and rushes at the tiger with no regard for his own safety. All he knows is that he hates the way Maulbreath always demolishes his teammates.

As he rears his stick back to fire at the puck, Maulbreath has no idea the mouse is racing at him. He swings his stick and still nails the puck, but he's taken by total surprise when Liten levies a massive hit that rocks him off his feet.

The puck flies at Harlan. The Gamblers goalie closes his eyes but manages to stay outside of his shell. He puts his gloved flipper out in the direction of the flying puck. Accident or not, he catches it.

As bad as the game is going, and as much as Safari Chip doubted his team earlier, he's encouraged to see some positive changes. Throughout the game, the Gamblers show spurts of great play and spurts of old play.

Kane gets penalties called against him as every third hit or so still seems to be illegal, but he manages to keep from being thrown out of the game. Rodman and Maulbreath get into another fight. Liten stays strong against the goons on the other team, but both he and Lovey take more than their fair share of violent checks. Tired from killing penalties, when the Gamblers do gain control of the puck, they mostly just dump it into their offensive zone so they can make line changes, losing the puck in the process.

The final score is 7-1 in favor of the Potatoes. After the game, the Gamblers shake hands and high-five the not so friendly Potatoes. Maulbreath gives a stinging high five to Rodman.

Inside the locker room, the Gamblers sit around looking dejected. They know they could have done better. The real let down for them, even more so than the score, is that they hit the ice with such high hopes, and they know they didn't play to their true potential.

Safari Chip stands before them with folded arms. "What was that?"

No one answers.

"It looked more like Monday Night Raw than a hockey game to me. Undertaker got thrown out of the game in the first minute, Rodman got two fighting penalties, Kane had ten penalties, and Liten and Lovey had their clocks cleaned as retaliation all game long."

The Gamblers stare at the floor humbled and embarrassed.

"I don't want to see anything like that ever again," Safari Chip warns.

Each player takes a turn apologizing to Safari Chip. No one looks him in the eye.

Suddenly, a smirk washes over Safari Chip and his attitude changes. "Now let's talk about the improvements. Rodman scored a goal, and we had the lead for a minute."

"Yeah!" Rodman shouts enthusiastically.

"We all saw Harlan catch the puck in his glove and not flinch a muscle. And you did that a bunch tonight Harlan. You didn't stay upright the entire game, but you've improved five hundred percent. Keep it up," Safari Chip continues.

Harlan smiles bashfully and nods at his coach.

"Kane!" Safari Chip shouts and turns to his Shih-Tzu. "Although you had ten penalties tonight, you *only* had ten penalties. That's down from the twenty-two you average per game."

Kane barks with a dangly tongue.

"Undertaker, you got thrown out and didn't play much, but I think you now understand what not to do," Safari Chip says.

"I do Chip," Undertaker says.

"Liten, I saw lots of improvement in your game with Kane out there. You even went right after Maulbreath. Now, if we can get Kane and Undertaker to protect you all game long, you're going to be back to all-star status in no time."

Liten points to both dogs, and they point back.

"Lovey, you've really turned up your game now that you've taken over for Sammie." Safari Chip points at his new starting winger.

"Thanks," Lovey replies.

"Speaking of Sammie, where is he? Will he be coming back?" Liten asks.

Safari Chip shrugs. "That's up to Sammie."

*

After hearing about all the improvements they've made, the Gamblers feel so good that they head out for a celebration dinner at the finest restaurant in the New Orleans Hotel.

Each of the Gamblers is dressed in something definitive to their character. Rodman wears one of his trademark Hawaiian shirts. Undertaker wears a black t-shirt with white bones piled up along the bottom. Kane's shirt is red with black flames. Lovey wears a plain black t-shirt and tie-dyed bandana around his head. Harlan's t-shirt reads FIVE HOLE. Maverick and Goose wear t-shirts that bear their colleges. The very proper Liten wears khaki pants and a dark blue dress shirt. Safari Chip was invited but declined as he has much planning to do for the upcoming game against the Utah Thumpers. The Gamblers eat and joke and laugh the night away.

Rodman stands and holds up a glass of passion fruit juice. He taps it with a fork, drawing the attention of his teammates. "Hey guys. Chip is right about us showing improvements. I think we're just a few games away from turning the corner to becoming a really good team."

There's a rowdy uproar of approval. Everyone high fives their nearest teammate.

"But don't forget, it's going to take a lot of hard work and continuous practice," Rodman continues.

"We don't mind practicing," Lovey says.

"Yes. It will be good to not be the laughing stock of the league anymore," Liten adds.

There's another uproar of approval.

Behind them, Sammie walks into the restaurant with a female koala. Liten is the first to notice him. He taps Rodman on the shoulder and points Sammie out. Rodman hopes Sammie's presence won't be a distraction to their good time. The other players see Rodman looking distractedly away and follow his gaze. They all see Sammie, who takes notice of them as well, though he walks arrogantly past their table pretending not to see them.

Rodman tries to refocus his team. "We've got a game tomorrow against the Utah Thumpers, and curfew is coming up, so we better wrap this up. I want you guys to know that no matter what happens this season, I'm proud of this team, and I'm proud to be a Gambler." He holds out his glass, and they all tap their glasses together.

The Gamblers finish their meal and head out of the restaurant. None of them notice Jason sitting on a bench just outside the restaurant. He holds a magazine over his face to disguise himself. Once the Gamblers pass him, he heads into the restaurant.

Sammie sits at a table across from his date. Over the top of the table, he holds her paws in his and looks into her eyes. "It's so good to not have to worry about going to practice and getting beat up in games Meggy Meg. Now, I can spend more time having fun with you."

Meggy Meg giggles.

Jason pulls up a chair and sits down uninvited.

The disturbance agitates Sammie. He grows even more upset when he sees Jason. "Hey! What's this?"

"I heard you got suspended," Jason says smugly.

"So what?" Sammie asks.

Jason looks over at Meggy Meg, clearly uncomfortable with her presence. "Do me a favor toots and beat it for a minute."

"Don't talk to her that way. Who do you think..."

"A friend," Jason answers Sammie's question before it's asked. "I don't mean to be rude, but I have a proposition for you." Jason turns to Meggy Meg. "May we have a moment in private?"

Meggy Meg looks to Sammie.

He frowns but nods at her.

"Whatever." Meggy Meg gets up and leaves.

Jason waits to speak until he sees Meggy Meg completely disappear from sight. He wants to make absolutely sure they're alone. His proposition for Sammie is not only completely immoral and devious, but it also one hundred and ten percent violates IAHL law. "I need your help. The Gamblers are slowly improving, and I want to put a stop to it."

"What do you want me to do about it? I don't even play for them anymore," Sammie says.

"But you could. If you wanted to, you could rejoin the team and sabotage them from the inside. I figure after the way they treated you, you might want some revenge." Jason wears his same old evil grin.

"Not really. I'm having a blast without them."

Jason is taken slightly aback. He was sure Sammie would help him. Set back but not defeated, he stands up from the table and throws down a card. "Well if you change your mind that's my card. Give me a call. I'm prepared to offer you a handsome reward, as well as a contract with the best team in the IAHL next season, if you do this. Think about it kid."

As Jason walks confidently away from the table, Sammie picks up the card and examines it thoughtfully.

Maybe revenge against the Gamblers would be fun.

Chapter 9: Overtime

The Gamblers battle to get the puck out of their zone, but the Utah Thumpers make the task a hard one. With only forty seconds left in the game, the score is 3-2 in favor of Utah.

Harlan has played phenomenally, blocking thirty of thirty-three shots. Rodman has two assists. Undertaker and Kane, the goal scorers, have served only three penalties a piece and have played stellar defense throughout. Lovey and Liten's play from start to finish has been exceptional, especially on the penalty kill. And still, after all their good play, the Gamblers find themselves down by one.

Undertaker battles a raccoon for the puck along the boards. Another Thumpers player and Lovey join the battle. The huddle of players creates a log jam and brings a temporary halt to the action.

"Kick it here Undertaker," Rodman calls from Undertaker's left.

Undertaker pushes his leg through the mess of sticks and limbs. He digs out the puck with his skate and kicks it out of the pile to Rodman.

Rodman corrals the puck on a bounce and races down ice to the Thumpers net. Three defenders skate backwards and in front of him. Rodman dekes the first and squeezes between him and the second. He whizzes around the third defender with a spin move, leaving an open lane to the net. As he moves towards the goalie, he trips on the skate of the last defender and falls on his belly.

Holding his stick out in front of him as he slides, Rodman manages to maintain control of the puck, maneuvering it left and right as he slides towards the net. Just before he passes the net, he flips the puck over and past the kneeling goalie.

The goal lights go off.

The game is tied 3-3 with twenty-six seconds left.

Behind the play, Undertaker and Kane come to an ice shaving halt.

"That guy is one bad mamajama," Kane says.

"That's why they call him Hott Rod," Undertaker says, and both dogs skate to celebrate with Rodman.

"Way to go Rodman!" Liten hops up to slap Rodman's helmet.

"Thanks man. It's not over yet though. There are twenty-six seconds left." Rodman downplays his goal. He doesn't want his teammates to settle for coming close.

The Gamblers and Thumpers finish out the game trying their best to score but neither does. The Gamblers are assured at least one point in the standings as each win is worth two points, losses in regulation are worth no points, but overtime and shootout losses are worth one point.

The horns in the arena resonate, and the speakers boom as the announcer addresses the crowd. "After three periods of hockey, the score is Utah 3, Las Vegas 3. After a sixty second intermission, the game will be decided in a five minute sudden death overtime."

The Gamblers skate to their bench. They sit and rest or grab a drink and receive last minute instructions from Safari Chip. In a flash, the buzzer sounds and intermission ends.

Rodman lines up across from the Thumpers center, an armadillo, for the first overtime faceoff. Rodman makes darn sure to win the faceoff, even falling to a knee to get the drop on the puck and block the armadillo out once the referee drops the puck.

Both teams play strong defense, and the five minute overtime expires with neither team having scored.

The arena announcer booms again. "At the end of overtime, the score remains Utah 3, Las Vegas 3. The game will now be decided in a best of five shootout."

The Gamblers nerves shake, feet tap, knees bump, and their hands, wings, hooves, paws, and flippers wiggle as they wait for their first shootout of the season.

From the ice, the referees call for the Gamblers first shooter.

Safari Chip turns to his bench. "Go get 'em Lovey."

Lovey jumps off the bench, hurtles the wall, and skates to a waiting puck at center ice. He has little hesitation as he grabs the puck and races towards the Utah goalie. He dekes left then right. He skates so close to the goalie that he has to fire the puck at the very last second. Still, he makes one last deke, faking the goalie out with what looks like a shot at the five hole. Then, he sends it top shelf over the goalie's shoulder into the net. Lovey pumps his fist and glides on one knee towards the boards.

Up 1-0 in the shootout, the Gamblers bench goes nuts.

The Thumpers send out their hard shooting armadillo. He takes the puck towards Harlan and blasts a shot so hard it sends Harlan retreating into his shell and the puck into the net.

The Gamblers groan, but Safari Chip doesn't let them languish. He sends Liten out and tells him to put them back on top.

Liten climbs over the bench wall to the ice. He takes a second to survey his surroundings. There are no cats, hedgehogs, ravens, or other vicious animals to distract him as he moves in on goal. This should be easy. He grabs the puck and moves in fast. As he approaches shooting range, he rears back and fakes a shot. The goalie dives to block the fake shot, falling to his tummy, and Liten easily taps the puck into the wide open net.

The Gamblers bench goes bananas again.

The Thumpers next shooter, a kangaroo, moves in on goal. He skates slow and methodically, but he fires a sudden lightning quick shot at Harlan, who although he's able to stays out of his shell, is unable to stop the puck.

Safari Chip sends out Kane next. The tallest player on the team throws one hind legs over the wall with ease and then the other. His eyes are huge and crazed as he approaches the waiting puck. They wobble like a bobblehead doll. He's a dog possessed as he moves in on goal. He doesn't bother to deke or fake a shot. He just blasts a shot through the five hole from about fifteen feet in front of the net that puts the Gamblers back up 3-2.

Once again, the Gamblers bench goes crazy.

The Thumpers send their grizzly cub to shoot next. On his approach to the net, he growls so loud it makes Harlan flinch. He sees the turtle flinch, so once he's close to the net, he snarls angrily and startles Harlan again. He uses his intimidation to blast a shot past the Gamblers goalie, tying the shootout once more.

"Put the nail in the coffin Undertaker," Safari Chip orders.

Undertaker hops the wall. Like Kane, he takes the puck down the ice without any trickery or pizzazz. He blasts a shot from just beyond the blue line so hard it whizzes past the goalie before he can even pick up the puck's trajectory.

As usual, the Gamblers bench is excited.

Even Safari Chip is excited. He turns to Rodman. "We need Harlan to make a save."

The Thumpers send their zebra to take the next shot. Rodman turns his attention to Harlan and whistles. Somehow, over the noise of the crowd, Harlan hears the whistle and looks to Rodman. With his lighthearted smile, Rodman points at his goalie and in one motion changes the point to a thumbs up.

Harlan shoots Rodman a thumbs up back.

Rodman quickly points towards the zebra, who has already started down the ice.

Harlan calmly pulls his mask down and settles in. He watches the zebra deke left, deke right, deke back left, and deke right again. Despite his cool head, Harlan gets tangled up in his own feet. He stumbles just before the zebra shoots the puck.

The zebra sees him falling and aims a shot high.

In a desperate maneuver, Harlan twists as he falls to his tummy and raises his stick in the air. As it happens, he places the stick in perfect position to block the puck and knock it down, denying the Thumpers a fourth goal.

The Gamblers bench goes extra wild now that they have a 4-3 lead. If their final shooter can score a goal, they'll win the game. If he misses, however, the Thumpers will have a chance to tie the shootout and send the game into a sudden death shootout.

The Gamblers don't sweat though. They have Rodman as their final shooter.

Safari Chip grabs Rodman by the shoulders. "Ok Rodman. This is it. You can seal the win with a goal here."

"You can count on me," Rodman guarantees.

As Rodman is announced, the crowd goes berserk.

Rodman jumps over the wall and takes his time skating to center ice. He stops behind the puck and takes a look around the rowdy crowd. This is his big chance to give them what they've been waiting for, what they expect of him.

He turns his attention to the Thumpers goalie, who shifts his skates left and right in preparation of Rodman's approach. Rodman raises a mischievous eyebrow in the goalie's direction and pounces on the puck. He skates fast, deking left and right. He glides along the ice with impeccable grace, handling the puck with the utmost skill. He sees where he wants to shoot the puck, but he makes sure not to eyeball the spot and give it away to the goalie. He maneuvers into perfect position to take his shot. Just a few more strides and he'll score. Just when things are looking too easy, the puck hits a divot in the ice, causing Rodman to lose control of it. The puck gets hung up and dribbles behind him, though Rodman himself keeps moving forward.

"Oh no!" whispers Safari Chip on the bench.

While Safari Chip and the rest of the Gamblers panic, Rodman recovers. He brings his stick around his back with his left flipper and regains control of the puck. Then, he secures the stick with his right flipper and looks back up as he rapidly approaches the goalie.

Confused at the awkward angle in which Rodman comes at him, the goalie gets into the best position he can, but he still can't see the puck. Rodman glides in front of him, spreads his legs, and shoots the puck from behind himself, between his legs, through the five hole.

The goal light goes off.

The Gamblers win.

The crowd jump out of their seats and go ape.

The Gamblers fly off the bench in a race to join a fist pumping and joyously screaming Rodman on the ice. Even Harlan races to the celebration, throwing down his stick, his gloves, and his helmet on the way.

Lovey reaches Rodman first. He jumps in the air and Rodman tries to catch him, but they still fall to the ice. Undertaker and Kane join in next and make it a dog pile. Liten, Maverick, and Goose all follow.

At the bottom of the pile, Rodman is all smiles and laughs. "This is it guys. We're a force to be reckoned with!"

Harlan, the last to join, jumps on top of the pile and spots a glimpse of Rodman at the bottom. "Rodman!"

"Harlan!" Rodman screams back.

"Gamblers!" Liten screams.

"Gamblers!" they all scream in unison.

*

Sammie sits at the juice bar inside the Mardi Gras Room watching the game on TV. He's unimpressed by the Gamblers victory, but he's still so unnerved by it that when Meggy Meg asks him to dance with her he refuses.

"I'm going to dance by myself then." Meggy Meg makes her way to the dance floor.

Sammie goes back to his bowl of eucalyptus leaves and his green tea. Next to him, a couple of pigeons have been watching the game since the start.

"That Rodman looks like the real deal," one pigeon says.

"Yeah, and it looks like he the rest of these guys might turn out to be real hockey players too," the other says.

"Where's Sammie Lou though?" the first inquires.

Neither pigeon notices Sammie sitting nearby in his sharp suit and dark sunglasses.

"I hear he quit the team," pigeon two answers.

"You don't say. My my. Well that's a shame."

"Yeah, but you see that new kid they got playing in place of him? Lovey. He's awesome."

"Yeah, and I guess they weren't winning with Sammie. Maybe change is good."

Sammie cringes as his ego takes a battering. He takes Jason's card out of his pocket, looks it over, and taps it against the bar.

*

In their locker room, the Gamblers dance to Lovey's boombox. The team circles around Rodman as he shows off, doing dances like the Roger Rabbit, the Running Man, and the Electric Slide. He finishes with a Moonwalk across the locker room to hoots, hollers, and cheers from the rest of the team.

Undertaker laughs so hard he falls to the ground and rolls around, and Kane has to hold onto a locker for support from laughing so hard.

Safari Chip has never seen a group this excited about one win. But, he knows it's not just the win. It's the confidence in themselves that has them so energized. He's excited too. "Hey fellas!" he hollers over the music.

The Gamblers turn their attention to their coach, but they don't stop dancing.

"I don't mean to interrupt the celebration, but I wanted to say that this was the best game you guys have played all year," Safari Chip tells them.

The Gamblers stop dancing for a moment to clap and cheer.

"As long as you continue to play like this, we're going to finish this season strong. And there's no doubt in my mind that with hard work, a lot of practice, and a lot of grinding out games we can make it to the championship game," Safari Chip continues.

The team cheers again and goes right back to dancing. They motion for Safari Chip to join in. He waves them off, but they insist. Maverick and Goose drag him into the center of the circle with Rodman and Harlan.

Rodman and Harlan try to encourage him as they dance, but Safari Chip is hesitant.

"Like this," Rodman says and shows Safari Chip some moves.

Safari Chip moves like Rodman and Harlan, clumsily at first, but the more he moves, the better and better he gets. His team might not think it, but he's done this before. He just needed to get warmed up. Soon, he's throwing down funky break dance moves like no other and steals the show. Rodman and Harlan are forced to back off and let the crazy monkey do his thing.

Jaws all around the locker room drop just long enough to be astonished, but eventually they all join in the boogie.

Chapter 10: The Season Shapes Up

When the Gamblers signed Rodman, their record was zero wins, eight loses, two overtime losses, and no shootout losses, or 0-8-2-0. Their record at that point totaled only two points in the official standings. Since getting Rodman, they have lost two more games but also won a game, improving to 1-10-2-0. The win doubles their points total in the standings from two to four. More impressive is that they doubled their points in less than half the games it took them to get their first two points. Still in last place, they find solace in the fact that they're adding to their wins and points.

After their win over the Thumpers, the Gamblers hit the road for their first road game with Rodman. He dons his white road jersey with black trim outlined in gold and red for the first time. Instead of the colliding red dice logo on front, GAMBLERS is spelled out in red letters outlined in black. The letters rest across a patch that resembles the Las Vegas sign.

Their first game is against the Stockton Lightning. The Gamblers continue to improve as they win their first game in regulation. Rodman and Liten score two goals apiece. Harlan stops twenty-two of twenty-six shots. Undertaker and Kane cut their penalties down to three a piece. Maverick and Goose provide solid minutes while giving the starters a breather here and there. And Lovey gets three assists and the game winning goal in the 5-4 win.

The Gamblers play back to back games against the Lightning and win them both. They are still in last place with a record of 3-10-2-0, but they have upped their points in the official standings from four to eight and are just four points behind the seventh place Ontario Californians.

After Stockton, the Gamblers head to Bakersfield, California to take on the Trains. The Gamblers control the game against the Trains from the opening faceoff when Rodman hits the puck back to Kane, who takes it down the ice and passes it to Liten.

Liten takes the puck over the blue line and comes to sudden halt near the net, sending so many chips of ice flying up from the rink that no one sees him pass the puck backwards to Undertaker near the blue line.

Undertaker blasts a shot past the confused Trains goalie, giving the Gamblers a one goal lead just eleven seconds into the game.

Their second goal comes after Kane is sent to the penalty box. On the penalty kill, Harlan stops a shot, and the puck is collected by Rodman.

Instead of just clearing the puck, Rodman heads for the other end of the ice. Two Trains defenders barrel down on him from either side in an attempt to keep their power play from being disrupted, but Rodman turns on his jets and whizzes past the oncoming attackers. In turn, the defenders run into each other and fall down, leaving Rodman alone on a breakaway.

The Trains goalie comes out too far in anticipation of Rodman's shot. Rodman dekes the goalie, causing him to dive prematurely and fall down, leaving the net wide open. Rodman holds the puck close to himself, swerves around the fallen goalie, and scores easily. He holds a knee to his tummy and pumps a fist as he glides away from the net.

The Gamblers get another goal when Liten clears the puck just as Kane is let out of the penalty box. Kane grabs the loose puck, rushes up on the goalie all alone, and blasts a shot the goaltender has absolutely no hope of stopping.

Harlan stops all but one of the Trains fourteen shots, and the Gamblers win 3-1. Even more impressive is the defense by the Gamblers to only allow the Trains to take fourteen shots.

*

Sammie continues to dance his nights away at the Mardi Gras Room. The two pigeons, along with the orangutan waiter at the juice bar, and another patron, an ostrich, continue to watch the Gamblers progress on TV. Convinced the Gamblers recent surge is still meaningless, Sammie dismisses the small gathering and lets them waste their time.

*

On the first game of the Gamblers next road trip, Rodman wakes up in a room not nearly as cozy as the one the Gamblers set him up in. Each morning, he and his road trip roommate, Lovey, have the same routine. Rodman grabs the complimentary newspaper from the front door, he and Lovey order room service, they sit at their breakfast bar, and read the sports page to see how they're doing in the standings. Today, it shows the Gamblers have climbed out of the cellar into seventh place with a 7-14-2-3 record for a total of eighteen points.

*

Jason and the Gold Rush hold a players only meeting prior to their next home game against the Gamblers. Each of the players sits at a desk in the conference room used to review tape.

"We have the Gamblers tonight. I don't know about you guys, but I'm not in the mood to get beat up again."

The Gold Rush players remain stone faced and intent as they listen to Jason.

"We need to go out there and show these Gambler punks that we're not going to put up with any shenanigans. We have to put them back in their place. Remind them that they still can't measure up to us. No one cares about their recent surge. We're the best team in the league. We're the best team in the world. We beat the pants off of them in the first game, and I say we give them an even bigger whooping tonight."

The Gold Rush players all make fists and pound their tables to show unification and camaraderie.

*

The Gamblers have a tough time with the Gold Rush. Undertaker and Kane pile up the penalties. They retaliate against the hard and dirty hitting of the Gold Rush. Their penalties leave the Gamblers on the penalty kill much of the time. As a result, the other Gamblers wear out quickly. Harlan ducks into his shell a lot. The hard shooting of the Gold Rush is tougher to handle than what he faces from other teams. Liten tries to stand his ground against Metz and Packer, but without Undertaker or Kane to back him up, the Gold Rush cats manhandle, or in this case mouse-handle, him from start to finish.

At one point, Rodman finds himself fighting for a puck along the boards with Rapture. As they fight for the puck, Jason comes from behind and smashes Rodman against the glass, causing his vision to go totally black with a few bright bursts or color like fireworks. His hearing leaves him momentarily too, and he falls limply to the ice dazed.

Undertaker and Kane skate into the play and push Rapture away from Rodman. They also grab Jason, who puts up a feeble fight, and they push him away too.

Jason receives a five minute boarding penalty. He doesn't mind though as he skates to the penalty box with a smile.

Rodman, meanwhile, needs the dogs' help to get to the bench.

On the power play, the Gamblers get just three shots and no goals in the first four minutes. The final shot results in a rebound off Haas' pads that gets collected by Iggy and taken down the ice for a shorthanded goal.

Jason laughs his head off in the penalty box.

Having seen enough of the reprehensible play and poor sportsmanship displayed by the Gold Rush, Rodman forces himself back onto the ice for the final minute of the power play. His presence on the ice draws enough attention away from the other Gamblers to enable them to get off some quick passes that eventually end with Liten shooting and scoring.

Still, after sixty minutes of hockey, the final score is 5-1 in favor of the Gold Rush. The Gamblers shake hands with the

Gold Rush after the game, but Jason, again, skates away before he reaches Rodman.

The Gold Rush leave the ice in high spirits and a lot less beat up after this game.

The Gamblers leave the ice eager to get on a plane back home.

*

Sammie sits at the juice bar inside the Mardi Gras Room. His obnoxious laughing at the Gamblers loss draws the ire of the pigeons, the orangutan, and the ostrich watching with him. They sneer at Sammie, giving him the reaction he wants, and he spits his tongue out at them.

*

Back home, the Gamblers regroup. Their first game is against the new worst team in the league, the Ontario Californians, but the game is far from easy. The Californians take an early two goal lead. Harlan remains outside his shell on each of the shots, but they still get past him, and the Gamblers don't score in either of the first two periods.

During the second intermission, Safari Chip bribes his team with a promise to make his world famous, highly coveted, Double Double Bonus Banana Split Sundaes for them if they can pull out a win. With the exception of Rodman, each player has experienced only a handful of these banana splits. Safari Chip uses them as incentive to sign players who might otherwise be reluctant and to get players to try extra hard at practice or games. Rodman doesn't understand why it's such a big deal, but the other players assure him the extra effort is worth the delicious treat.

The Gamblers go out and dominate the third period. Harlan makes eye-popping save after eye-popping save. Liten, an ice-cream aficionado, scores the first goal unassisted.

Maverick ties the game with a rare goal of his own on an assist by Rodman and Lovey.

At this point, the Californians look as though they know there's nothing they can do to win this game. They stare stunned, breathing hard, and sweating up a storm across the ice at the poised and focused Gamblers.

The Gamblers know there's no way they won't win this game or their Double Double Bonus Banana Split reward.

To further encourage his team, Safari Chip gives them one more stipulation. During a break in the game, he informs his team that in order to receive their ice-cream treat, they must win in regulation.

Liten's eyes go wide with panic. He wants that banana split.

With only a minute and change left in the game, Rodman loses the next faceoff.

The Californians left winger, a black panther, takes the puck towards Harlan. The Californians try to set up in the Gamblers zone, but the panther is brutally checked against the glass by Liten and loses the puck.

Kane swoops in, snags the loose puck, and leads the Gamblers across the blue line the other way. They successfully gain the zone and set up. The Gamblers have the Californians outnumbered as the panther recovers from the vicious hit he took at the other end of the ice.

Liten skates behind the net and clacks his stick against the ice to let Kane know he's open. Kane passes the puck Liten's way. It almost gets picked off. Luckily, Rodman bumps the defender, gets his stick on the puck first, spins, and passes it blindly in front of the net.

Liten takes the goalie by surprise, skating out from behind the net. He dings the puck in for the go-ahead and eventual game winner. The Gamblers race to join him in celebration in front of the net, but Liten races to the bench instead

"All vanilla ice-cream Chip! I want all vanilla ice-cream on my spilt!" Liten's eyes are crazy and his tone serious.

Safari Chip chuckles. "Ok. All vanilla ice-cream for Liten. But there are still eleven seconds left. Go finish this thing."

Rodman wins the next faceoff. Liten makes sure to be the one with puck. The Californians chase him, but he plays keep away, killing the remaining seconds and securing a 3-2 Gamblers win.

*

In a game the Gold Rush are losing to the Idaho Potatoes, Jason looks up at the out-of-town scoreboard and sees the Gamblers have won another game. He's disgruntled and takes his frustrations out on Lance Maulbreath with a crosscheck. Whistles blow and he receives a penalty. Jason goes to the penalty box and slams his helmet on the ground, making the penalty box attendant uncomfortable.

After calming down a bit, Jason stares the attendant down, but the attendant avoids eye contact with the angry penguin.

"Hey pops! I need to make a phone call," Jason grumbles.

"Here?" the attendant asks.

"Yeah here."

"You want to make a call while in the penalty box?" The attendant has never heard of a player making phone calls from within the penalty box. It's probably against IAHL rules.

"That's what I said. Do you have a phone or what?" Jason asks.

The attendant pulls out his cell phone and hands it over. At the moment, Jason is scarier than the possibility of being reprimanded by the league.

Jason flips his gloves off and dials Sammie. It rings and rings and rings, but Sammie doesn't answer. Jason flips the phone closed and tosses it back to the attendant carelessly. He sighs heavily and then kicks a dent into the penalty box wall.

*

The Gamblers keep rolling. Before a rare afternoon game, they sit around the locker room eating the biggest most delicious banana splits ever. Rodman has the sports page open. He points out to his teammates their 11-16-2-4 record and twenty-eight points. More importantly, he points out the fact that they have leapfrogged another team.

That night, the Trains deliver the Gamblers a setback. They punish the Gamblers in a 7-1 rout. The Gamblers suffer the ill effects of massive tummy aches from finishing every last bite of their Double Double Bonus Banana Spilt Sundaes before the game. Throughout the game they feel sick, heavy, and weighed down.

Safari Chip makes a new team rule after the game. No more sundaes before games.

The Gamblers rebound in their next game. Against the Victoria, British Columbia, Canada Fishermen, they win in a rout of their own. The final score is 6-0. Harlan has to work harder than ever, but he stops a season and career high forty-five shots for his first ever shutout.

Rodman skates to Harlan after the final buzzer and puts his flipper around the goalie. He points to the word SHUTOUT flashing across the scoreboard.

The normally leafy green cheeks on Harlan's face turn bright red.

Aside from Harlan's record setting shutout, there's another record set. Undertaker and Kane have a shutout of their own so to speak. It's the first game in which neither dog goes to the penalty box.

The Gamblers get a goal and an assist from each of their starting five players and at least one point from each player on the team as Gooses adds the sixth goal of the game on an assist from Maverick and Harlan. The horse and goose, though not starters, have great chemistry when on the ice together.

It's a big win over a good team.

After a short and successful road trip, the Gamblers head home for two games and then right back out on the road. In another hotel room, Rodman eats a bowl of cereal with one flipper and reads the sports page with the other. Lovey reads over his shoulder. The Gamblers have climbed into fifth place with a 17-19-4-4 record and forty-two points.

"We almost have as many wins as losses," Lovey remarks.

"Two more games and I guarantee we'll be there," Rodman says. They finish their breakfast and head to practice.

*

Just as Rodman predicted, the Gamblers do win their next two games. They win three and then four and then five games in a row until they've won eight straight games. Gamblers 2, Thumpers 1. Gamblers 4, Potatoes 1. Gamblers 5, Lightning 3. Gamblers 2, Fishermen 0. Gamblers 6, Californians 4. Gamblers 2, Trains 1. Gamblers 4, Lightning 2. Gamblers 4, Thumpers 2. The wins pile up.

The stats start to pile up too. Rodman moves into the IAHL's top five in points, and Lovey moves into the top five in assists. Both Gamblers make a strong case for the rookie of the year award. Harlan's save percentage heads in the upward direction. Prior to Rodman's arrival, Harlan's percentage of blocked shots was a minuscule eight percent. Since Rodman's arrival and the practice Harlan's put in, his percentage has climbed to eighty-two percent. Once they are able to stay out of the penalty box, Undertaker and Kane find themselves rapidly approaching the top of the leader board for hits and blocked shots.

Rodman sits with the rest of the team huddled around him looking at the standings. With a 29-25-4-5 record and sixty-seven points, they have jumped two spots into a tie for third with the Fishermen. To make the championship game, the Gamblers need to finish in second place or higher. They are eight points behind the second place Idaho Potatoes, but they have nine games left in their season.

The Gold Rush, as usual, are in first place by a mile over everyone.

The standings have the Gamblers fired up as they exit the locker room and head to the ice for their game with the only team they have zero wins against this season, the Gold Rush.

After watching the Gamblers get better and better without him, Sammie ponders Jason's offer more and more. He goes to watch the game from the crowd to get a better sense of whether or not he wants to agree to join Jason in his plan, and he has to admit that likes what he sees in the play of the Gold Rush. But, he sees that the Gamblers are still no match for the Alaska team. Sammie leaves halfway through the 8-3 romp and decides to leave the Gamblers alone and worry about his hockey future next season.

After the game, the Gold Rush laugh in the faces of the Gamblers as they shake hands. Jason, as usual, skips out of line before he gets a chance to shake with Rodman.

"One day we'll learn how to beat those guys, but until then, we have to keep playing smart hockey," Safari Chip warns his depressed team in their locker room.

*

The season continues on for the Gamblers, one win after another. They win the following seven games after their most recent loss to the Gold Rush. As the season comes to its final game, the Gamblers find themselves tied with the Potatoes for second place, and as luck would have it, the teams play each other with the winner advancing to the championship game.

The Gamblers go up 1-0 on an early goal by Rodman. After his goal, the Potatoes are intent on getting back into the game and rev up their intensity. The Gamblers find it hard to do anything against them. They struggle to get the puck across their blue line, set up offense, get the puck out of their defensive zone, and in what seems like the blink of an eye, the Potatoes score twice to take a 2-1 lead just before the first period ends.

*

Jason and the Gold Rush intently watch the game between the Gamblers and the Potatoes in their locker room. They have already secured the first spot in the championship game and are eager to find out which team they'll face in the Cup Finals. Part of Jason doesn't want Rodman to ever even taste a championship game. Another part of him wants to pulverize, humiliate, and rub in the face of Rodman a championship win.

*

The Gamblers start the second period with more fire in their play. Undertaker and Kane check everything within a three foot radius clean and hard. Their hits take a toll on the Potatoes, and soon, the fire the Potatoes had finished the first period with turns to fumes, and the momentum swings back the Gamblers way.

As Maulbreath takes the puck down the ice, Liten pokes it away from the tiger, snags it with his own stick, stops on a dime, and heads in the opposite direction. He races away from Maulbreath as fast as he can skate, but the tiger is fast. He catches up to Liten and swipes at the mouse with a paw. Liten ducks out of the way just in time. He passes the puck to Kane, who slips the puck through the legs of a Potatoes defender, across the blue line, and then bowls the defender over.

Lovey secures the puck and sees Rodman behind the net. It appears to him that the Potatoes goalie has no idea of

Rodman's presence there because he never once turns to check Rodman down.

Suddenly, Rodman skates from behind the net to the side next to the goalie.

Lovey fires towards the net with a quickness and Rodman uses his stick to deflect and redirect the puck into the net for his second goal of the night. The Gamblers have a brief celebration, but they immediately get back to work.

After a hard fought twenty minutes, the second period ends in a 2-2 tie.

*

The Mardi Gras Room is a frenzy of excitement. Sammie tries to ignore the Gamblers supporters, but the animals dancing with him keep making their way to the juice bar to watch the pivotal game. As more and more animals leave the floor, the cheering gets louder.

Sammie's emotions overtake him. Not only are the Gamblers doing well without him and having a blast, they're stealing his good time at the Mardi Gras Room too. He pulls Jason's card from his pocket once more.

*

Very early in the third period, the Potatoes jostle for position in front of the Gamblers net. The Gamblers play very good defense, not allowing the Potatoes to have any openings on net. Maulbreath gets frustrated and whips a vicious slap shot at the net in an effort to create something. Somehow, the puck finds a hole all the way through traffic, past Harlan, and into the net for a goal.

Harlan shakes his head in disbelief. He wonders how he could let such a shot get by him.

The Gamblers play panicked for more than half of the period. They look sloppy on offense, rarely getting set up with an opportunity to develop a play and desperate on defense, just barely stopping several big plays from the sticks of Potatoes players.

With eight minutes to go and a break in the action, Safari Chip rallies his team at their bench. "Look guys, you have to settle down. Don't panic. You look like scared little mice out there…"

Liten clears his throat.

"Oops! Sorry Liten. But you guys look like you're playing as though your life depends on the outcome. You're passes aren't crisp, you're shots are off target, and your skating is shoddy. Some of you are skating as if it were the first time you'd ever even seen skates or ice. Relax. You play better when you're relaxed." Safari Chip stops talking and looks around at his team to see if they're listening to him.

They smile and nod uncomfortably.

"I'm serious. Loosen up!" Safari Chip demands.

Rodman does a quick full body shake. "I'm loose Chip."

"Yeah you are! You called me Chip!" Safari Chip playfully slaps Rodman's shoulder.

Liten shakes animatedly too and declares, "I too am loose Chip."

Undertaker and Kane hit each other with friendly paws. "We're loose Chip!"

Lovey does a perfect back flip on the ice, awing the bench and the crowd. "I'm loose Chip!"

And they are loose.

The head referee blows his whistle and calls both teams back to center ice.

*

Sammie finds himself dancing alone at the Mardi Gras Room. Even Meggy Meg has gone to the juice bar to watch the game. Having no fun at all, he pulls a cell phone from his pocket and dials Jason.

"Hello?" Jason answers.

"It's Sammie. Sorry it took so long, but I'm in."

Jason leans back in his chair tickled at the news. "Well, as it stands, it looks like we won't need your help."

"Nothing's over yet. But I guess if you want to take that chance…"

"Ok. Ok. Ok. Give me a call after the game. If the Gamblers win, we'll get together and discuss the specifics."

"Fine."

Jason smiles his rotten smile and hangs up.

*

Rodman wins the faceoff after the break. The Gamblers take the puck across the blue line and set up. They deliver a flurry of passes from one player to the next. Kane to Lovey. Lovey back to Kane. Kane to Undertaker. Undertaker to Liten. Liten to Rodman. Rodman back to the top with Kane.

All the passing gets the Potatoes crossed up, and the puck gets passed to Rodman. He races behind the net under the close watch of the Potatoes goalie. Rodman wraps around to his right, and though the goalie slides from one side of the net to the other, Rodman wins the race and scores his third goal of the night.

The score is tied again at 3-3.

Rodman skates to the glass and pounds it rapidly, celebrating with the fans pounding back on the other side. Soon, he's mobbed by his teammates, who tackle him to the ground. They scream and hug and scream some more.

Maulbreath scoffs at them from a distance.

The Gamblers get up one by one. Undertaker and Kane each grab one of Rodman's flippers to help him up.

*

The Mardi Gras Room goes nuts.

*

Above Rodman, on the giant arena screen, his picture is displayed with the words HAT TRICK. The Gamblers fans flood the ice with their hats. They throw thousands of hats in all different sizes, colors, and designs over the glass in honor of the feat. Their spur-of-the-moment celebration halts play while Gamblers personnel clear the ice.

The Gamblers skate to their bench, still celebrating with Rodman, patting him on the back and giving him high fives as they wait for play to resume. They laugh as a dozen workers use shovels and trash cans to remove over 7,000 hats from the ice.

Once the ice is clear, the referees give the signal for the Gamblers and Potatoes to head back to center ice. Adrenaline flows like a river through both teams. Rodman is so shaky that he loses the faceoff. He has to force himself to calm down and regain his composure as he joins his teammates in the play.

Time dwindles down to a few precious seconds, and the Gamblers regain control of the puck. They take a mass amount of shots on goal, but the Potatoes goalie manages to stop their onslaught.

Regulation ends with the score tied.

During the one minute break, Safari Chip reminds his team of their different jobs during overtime. He also reminds them to stay relaxed. Maverick and Goose take water bottles and squirt water into the mouths of the starting six to rehydrate them before the game resumes.

The minute goes by in a flash. The referees whistle for both teams.

Rodman lines up across from Maulbreath.

The puck is dropped.

Rodman wins, but gets cross checked from behind by Maulbreath. The hit knocks him to the ice in pain.

Liten takes the puck to the offensive zone. His path gets blocked by one of the Potatoes defenders, and he's diverted directly into the path of Maulbreath. The tiger tries to swipe at Liten again, but the mouse ducks out of the way, so Maulbreath sticks his skate out and trips Liten to make sure the mouse doesn't get past him.

Whistles blow all over the ice.

Liten gets up and shoves the tiger. Maulbreath roars, shows his teeth, and swipes hard at Liten yet again. This time, he catches Liten square in the head, knocking him off his feet.

More whistles blow.

Liten lies motionless on the ice.

The Gamblers race to his aid. Undertaker and Kane jump Maulbreath from behind, and some of the Potatoes fight back.

Whistles blow from every direction. The referees have a hard time getting the mêlée under control. It's only with the help of Rodman, Lovey, and a few of the less aggressive Potatoes that everyone is separated.

After both teams are calmed down, the referees confer about who saw what and what penalties to assess. Meanwhile, Rodman and the Gamblers check on Liten. His face is scratched and bloodied. He's dazed but not seriously injured. Undertaker and Kane help him up and skate him to the bench.

The referees come for the dogs. They inform them that they're each to serve the remainder of the overtime in the penalty box for fighting. Maulbreath receives a ten minute game misconduct penalty and is also hit with a match penalty that carries with it an immediate removal from the game and a definite suspension. He's sent to the locker room and another of the Potatoes gets a five minute fighting penalty for his actions against Undertaker and Kane.

Each team sends two players to the penalty box for at least five minutes. Overtime is set to conclude with four on four. Because the dogs are in the penalty box and Liten is made to ride the bench while he recovers from whiplash, the Gamblers send out a lineup of all rookies, Rodman, Lovey and Goose up front with Maverick on defense.

Both teams play the final three plus minutes of overtime on their best behavior. Neither team scores. Another one minute break is given before the second overtime starts, because IAHL rules state that there are no shootouts in games that decide champions or trips to a championship game.

The second overtime starts with Liten back on the ice in place of Goose. Undertaker, Kane, and two Potatoes players, one of whom is serving Maulbreath's ten minute penalty, remain in the penalty box.

Rodman wins the fifth period's first faceoff, and the Gamblers head out on offense. They get a few shots on goal but are denied each time.

Ten seconds to go in the penalties.

The Potatoes gain control of the puck and head towards Harlan. One of their big shooters rears back and blasts a shot. It's the type of blast that still sometimes sends Harlan into his shell.

The Gamblers watch nervously, but the only part of Harlan that moves is his arm as it reaches over his shoulder and catches the puck. The rest of him stands firm. He flicks the puck out of his glove to Lovey, and Lovey passes it up to Rodman.

The penalties expire and Undertaker is allowed out of the box. Kane and the Potatoes player who got called for fighting aren't though, because Maulbreath's ten minute penalty puts the Gamblers on the power play, and if all three players were let out at once, there would be too many men on the ice.

*

Maulbreath watches the final moments of the game on TV in his locker room. He wishes he wouldn't have let his emotions get the better of him. He wants to be on the ice with his team, helping them, but all he can do now is hope his team scores first.

*

Rodman smacks a shot on goal. He misses by less than an inch, and the puck rings off the pole.

The crowd goes nuts.

The Potatoes goalie looks behind him to see if the puck went in. He can't find it.

The crowd is on the edge of their seats with excitement and disappointment at the narrow miss.

Liten collects the rebound and skates limply around the net.

The goalie checks Liten down, but he still can't find the puck. He can't tell whether or not Liten has it. He turns back to check the ice in front of the net and sees his teammates pointing and yelling, but he can't make out their words. He's completely and utterly confused until the goal light behind him starts flashing and spinning.

Liten falls to his belly drained and woozy from playing so hard while still suffering from his earlier attack. Rodman dives on his belly and slides to Liten. Undertaker, Lovey, and Maverick race to join the celebration. Kane comes out of the penalty box in time to catch up with Harlan and Goose, who make their way to another dog pile on the ice. Even Safari Chip makes his way to the celebration, though he stops to shake hands with the Potatoes coach.

*

Maulbreath slumps in his chair as he watches the celebration. Despite his anguish, he can't take his eyes off the TV.

*

The scoreboard flashes the final score. Gamblers 4, Potatoes 3. It also flashes the season's final standings. Alaska is in first with a record of 48-19-3-2, one hundred and one points and Las Vegas is in second with a record of 37-26-4-5, eighty-three points.

*

The Mardi Gras Room erupts in festive celebration. The pigeons high five each other and spill their juice all over the bar. A rat in the crowd jumps up and down elated and he spills his pretzels and peanuts on the floor. The orangutan pours everyone free juice. Several animals hug each other while others throw streamers and confetti.

*

In the Alaska locker room, the Gold Rush turn off the TV. Coil heads to his office to begin his game planning. He's not too threatened by the Gamblers since they haven't beaten his team once all season, but he's also not willing to take any chances by not preparing.

Jason remains unmoved in his seat, staring at the blank TV screen, grinning his same old rotten smile.

*

In South Africa, the Chill watch the conclusion of the game and go wild with delight at the fact that their old captain and former alternate have both led their new teams to the championship game.

"I wish we could have been there for this," Spoedige says.

"Well," says The Coach thoughtfully. "Why don't we head up there for the championship?"

"Serious?" Dolvy asks.

"Why not? It'll be fun, and we have a former player on each team. We should be there to show them our support."

"One of them anyway," Pikkewyn says.

*

On the ice, the Gamblers are each awarded an IAHL finalist t-shirt and a hat with theirs and the IAHL Finals logo. A red carpet stretches from the tunnel to center ice and leads to a table draped by red cloth. Upon the table sits the Martino Trophy. Each the first and second place teams receive this trophy to acknowledge their finish to the season and entrance. The Martino Trophy is a prelude to the bigger prize, the Anderson Cup. Both trophies are named after prominent IAHL founders and coaches, Snickers Doodle Anderson who was the first coach to lead his team to the championship, and Bartholomew Martino, the first runner up.

While the Gamblers await the presentation of their trophy, the arena announcer booms, "It's now time to announce the three stars of the game for *your Las Vegas Gamblers!*"

The crowd cheers.

"The third star in tonight's game, with twenty-eight saves and the win, *Harlan T. Turtle!*"

Harlan skates away from the trophy table towards the glass. He holds up a Gamblers t-shirt and waves it above his head. The crowd jumps and waves, trying to get his attention. He hurls the shirt as far into the crowd as he can to a couple of teenage beavers that jostle for it.

"The second star of tonight's game with the game winning goal, *Liten Mus!*"

Liten ventures to a different section of the arena. He tosses a shirt into the crowd to an attractive girl mouse a few rows behind the front row. He winks at her, and she blushes.

"And the first star of tonight's game…" the announcer pauses. "With a hat trick and an assist on the game winning goal…" he pauses again.

The crowd goes bonkers.

"*The captain! Rodman T. Penguin!*"

The cheering goes through the roof.

Rodman skates around, looking to hand his shirt to just the right animal. He finds a small Westie pup sitting in a wheelchair with a broken leg in the front row. The pup's eyes light up when Rodman points to him. "Do you have a pen?" Rodman calls to his mother.

"Pardon me?" she yells back.

"A pen?" Rodman yells louder and motions with his flipper like he's signing something.

She searches into her purse for a pen, finds one, and throws it to him. Rodman signs the shirt, throws it over the glass into the overjoyed pup's lap, gives him a wink and a thumbs up, and skates off to rejoin his team and the IAHL president at the trophy table.

The president congratulates the Gamblers on a fine season and presents them with the Martino Trophy. They pose for a picture with the trophy, but they make darn sure not to touch it. There's a superstition that if anyone on the team touches it, they'll jinx their chances at winning the Anderson Cup.

After all the interviews, celebrations with the crowd, and trophy presentations, the Gamblers head to the tunnel. They wave to their fans and high five those located near the tunnel entrance. None of them see Sammie high above the tunnel looking down on them with bitterness and disdain.

Chapter 11: Sammie's Bad News Plan

Plastic drapes cover the Gamblers lockers to protect the contents from becoming sticky with the forthcoming celebration. Dozens of bottles of sparkling juice await the team in giant plastic coolers filled with ice. Cameramen wait with their record buttons pressed. Reporters line the walls, waiting for the winning team to arrive so they can try to get interviews.

The locker room doors fly open. The Gamblers, led by Undertaker and Kane, rush in. They run straight for the coolers, grab, shake, and pop the tops of the bottles, sending juice and suds flying through the air. They aim their bottles and send juice flying all over the room and at each other.

Some of the more daring reporters make their way into the celebration, braving the splashing juice to get interviews. The players hoot, holler, squawk, bark, roar, squeak, and nay around the room and the cameras until the last bottle of juice is emptied and all are soaked and sticky. All in all, they keep the partying to a minimum. They know they have one more game to go.

After most of the reporters leave, most of the Gamblers hit the showers. Only Rodman remains in the locker room, answering questions for a final reporter that has been waiting patiently. Rodman's interviews go longer than the other players, a pleasant downside to being captain. By the time the interview wraps up, the other Gamblers have already returned from their showers and made their way to a table that has been set up with each player's favorite foods. The spread includes fish and peanut butter sandwiches, hotdogs, honey, fruit, oats, corn on the cob, and pizza.

Rodman skips his shower and just throws on a clean championship game shirt so he can joins his teammates at the feast.

Safari Chip finds himself alone with his team for the first time since winning a trip to the championship game. He stands before them with a grin a mile wide. He catches a banana thrown to him from the buffet spread. "Thanks Harlan."

Harlan winks at him.

"I have to tell you guys. I've never been more proud of a team I've been a part of. You played your hearts out this year," Safari Chip applauds.

The team cheers.

"Ok. Ok. Ok. You guys have your fun. I'm going to go start working on our game plan for the championship game," Safari Chip says.

"Coach," Rodman calls.

"Yeah?"

"I know we haven't beaten the Gold Rush once this season. And I know we haven't even kept the score close. But I know in my heart and in my head that we have the better team, the better coach, and more desire than any team has ever had. We can totally win this," Rodman says with the utmost conviction.

Safari Chip nods in acknowledgment.

The Gamblers break into more cheers.

The hustle and bustle of celebration only comes to a halt, and it's a screeching halt, when the locker room doors open unexpectedly, and in walks Sammie.

Sammie slowly makes his way towards his former teammates. "Hi Chip," he says as he passes him.

"Hi Sam," Safari Chip politely but suspiciously greets him back.

Sammie walks closer to the team. "Hi fellas."

Instead of a greeting back, Sammie's met by a disturbing silence.

"You're all probably wondering why I'm here. I know I acted like a jerk this season, and I was a big part of the problem holding this team back. For that I apologize. The crowd at the Mardi Gras Room watches your games every night. You should see how crazy that place goes when you guys win. I just wanted to tell you guys personally that I'll be rooting for you in the championship game." Sammie's words sound sincere despite his vile intentions, but he panics when none of the Gamblers have no response. He was hoping, a bit naively, that they would invite him back with open arms. He doesn't know how he's going to weasel his way back onto the team. "Well," he says with a heavy sigh and a frown. "I better get going." He turns and starts to walk out of the locker room.

"Wait," Rodman calls.

Sammie furrows his eyebrows and smiles maliciously. Bingo! He turns back to Rodman and the team, the look of utter depression and humiliation all over his face again.

"Listen. We all had things we needed to work on this season. Everyone in one way or another worked their problems out and has become a better player and teammate because of it. Sooo..." Rodman looks around at his teammates to see if they're thinking what he's thinking. "If it's all right with the rest of the guys, I'd like to welcome you back."

No one responds.

"That is as long as you promise you'll obey curfew and other team rules," Rodman adds.

"I'll be in bed early. I'll be the first guy on the ice and the last to leave," Sammie lies.

"What do you guys say? Can Sammie come back?" Rodman knows he'll need a unanimous vote.

The still silent room makes Sammie nervous. Many of the Gamblers faces remain uneasy.

Can Sammie be trusted? Should he be trusted? Should he be given a second chance to prove himself?

Finally, the silence is broken by Liten. As one of the alternate captains, he knows it's his job to back Rodman up whether he's right or wrong. "I do not see why not. We are going to need all the help we can get in the championship game."

"I'd like Sammie to come back too," Undertaker takes a cue from the two captains.

"Yeah. When he's awake, he's a really good player," Kane agrees.

Harlan perks up. "He's a good defender, and I could use all the defense I can get."

"Come on back Sammie," Goose squawks.

"Sammie's back," Maverick joins the welcome wagon.

The only player yet to answer is Lovey. He doesn't want to be selfish and be the only player to deny Sammie, but at the same time, he knows he took Sammie's spot, and he's worried if Sammie comes back, he'll lose his spot in the lineup. He's worked really hard all season to help get the Gamblers into the position they're in, and he doesn't want to give that up.

The team turns to Lovey for his answer.

Lovey looks awkwardly around at everyone. "Well," he hesitates. His sense of *team* kicks in. "Let's make it unanimous."

Everyone gets up from the buffet table. They shake hands with Sammie and welcome him back. They have no way of knowing, and no reason to think, that Sammie's return is going to be disaster for them. Instead, they rejoice in his return and lead him to the smorgasbord on the table.

Safari Chip watches his team, awed at their character for allowing Sammie a new start. He allows them to celebrate while he retreats to his office with his banana. They haven't accomplished their main goal, and he refuses to rest until they have the Anderson Cup in their locker room.

The Gamblers huddle around Sammie, tell him stories of their season, and ask him questions about what he's been up to. They tell him jokes, compliment his attire, and stuff food in his face. He finds it hard to be angry with them. Knowing he's about to sabotage these friendly animals makes him feel pretty lousy, and he decides he has to get away from the celebration.

"Hey everyone. I have to have a word with Chip. I'll be right back." Sammie makes his way to Safari Chip's office. Behind him, the Gamblers throw their championship game hats around the room in honor of Rodman's hat trick. Sammie walks into the office without knocking. "Hi Chip."

Safari Chip sits at his desk watching old footage. He pauses the tape and looks towards Sammie. "Hi Sam."

"I wanted to say thanks for you and the guys letting me come back."

"They're a good group of guys."

"I know." Sammie cringes.

"I have to tell you though." Safari Chip lays down his remote. "Even though you're back I'm going to start Lovey in the championship game. He's been working hard all season long."

Sammie's tummy drops. He never anticipated he might not be starting. How's he supposed to ruin the Gamblers if he's not in the game? "That's ok. I wouldn't want to come in and screw up everything you guys have done. I'm just glad to be back."

Safari Chip nods. "You're ok Sammie Lou."

"Thanks Coach."

Safari Chip goes back to watching old footage, and Sammie leaves his office. In the locker room, the rest of the team watches Rodman try to teach Liten to dance. They don't see Sammie slip into the hallway.

Sammie pulls out his cell phone and dials Jason. "Hello Jason? It's Sammie." Sammie checks the hallway to see if he's alone. The coast is clear. "Yeah. They took me back. Let's meet at the Mardi Gras Room tomorrow."

*

Sammie waits for Jason in a booth tucked away in a dark corner. To further conceal his identity, Sammie wears a fedora and dark sunglasses. He's petrified of getting caught and plays with his fingers nervously.

Jason enters the Mardi Gras Room and sneaks up on Sammie. "Boo," Jason whispers into Sammie's ear.

Sammie jumps out of his seat. He turns around and stares angrily at Jason. "Don't do that."

Jason laughs and takes a seat.

Sammie thought he'd feel better once he was away from the Gamblers hospitality and good will. As he sits with Jason though, he continues to feel like a heel.

"Wow. What a bunch of suckers. I knew they'd fall for it," Jason laughs.

"Yeah. They're pretty gullible," Sammie responds.

"What's wrong kid? You don't seem very excited."

"Well. Chip told me he's not starting me. He's going with Lovey since I wasn't there most of the season."

"I anticipated that could be a possibility. Don't worry. I'll get you in the game one way or another." Jason makes a fist and pounds it against his open flipper menacingly.

Sammie gulps back a heap of tension and reservation. He's a mess of confusion and uncertainty about whether or not ruining the Gamblers season is what he really wants. Perhaps his decision was made too hastily. It's too late now he thinks. He already told Jason he'd do it. Besides, if he makes Jason mad, Jason could get him into a lot of trouble with the league. He tries to remind himself that next year at this time he'll be having the time of his life as a Gold Rush, and all of this distress will be far behind him.

Chapter 12: Championship Day Pregame

The day of the championship game, a crowd the size of Mardi Gras itself swarms around the New Orleans Hotel. Thousands of animals revel in festivities that include hot dog vendors, live radio stations broadcasts, IAHL trivia contests, face painting booths, grilling in the parking lot, Gamblers look-a-like contests, and for a short while, the Gamblers themselves come out to sign autographs and take pictures with fans.

One of the IAHL rules is that the first place team does not host the championship game. The second place team gets home ice in an effort to level the playing field and make the game more exciting. The Gold Rush could care less where they play. They know they can beat anyone anywhere, anytime. They've already beaten the Gamblers five times in Las Vegas this season.

Almost everyone at the hotel wears Gamblers jerseys, t-shirts, sweatshirts, hats, headbands, sunglasses, tank tops, and skirts. A decent outpouring of Gold Rush fans are decked out in all the same attire baring their own team's logo. Despite the heated rivalry between the teams, Gamblers fans and Gold Rush fans alike get along like old friends.

The Coach, Spoedige, Pikkewyn, and Dolvy are amongst the crowd outside the hotel. They all wear Gamblers shirts and jerseys.

"Wow! Look at this crowd," Spoedige says.

"We never had anything like this in South Africa," Pikkewyn notes.

"This is the big leagues boys. That's what happens up here," The Coach says.

A wild and crazy girl penguin runs up to Dolvy and squawks loudly in his face. He jumps back, having the dickens scared out of him. Then, he's taken aback again as she throws her flippers around him and plants a big kiss on his beak. Afterwards, she runs away and disappears into the crowd. Dolvy and the others are left speechless.

"We never have anything like that in South Africa either," Pikkewyn says.

"Does that happen in the big leagues too Coach?" Spoedige asks.

"Ummm. That doesn't happen anywhere in real life," The Coach promises.

"But what..." Spoedige tries to ask.

"Don't ask kid," The Coach interrupts the potentially loaded question.

"Let's make our way inside. I don't want to miss any part of this." Dolvy wears a mile wide grin and moves through the crowd. The Chill follow him into the hotel where the party really rages.

*

Inside the Gamblers locker room, the team is relaxed. Each player partakes in leisurely activities to try and help them remain loose.

Safari Chip walks out of his office. It puts him at ease to see his team looking so much at ease. He makes his way to a table where Undertaker, Kane, and Liten play cards.

"Hey. You guys ready for the game?" Safari Chip asks.

"All ready Chip." Kane watches the hand between Undertaker and Liten.

"If tonight's game is as easy as this card game, we won't have any problem Chip," Undertaker jokes.

"Oh laugh it up you brute. You play cards like you play hockey. You are a bully. You probably have nothing at all." Liten slaps the table.

"Then why don't you make the call buddy?" Undertaker goads.

Liten thinks for a moment. He looks to Safari Chip and Kane for their thoughts.

They nod at him, saying go for it.

Liten studies his cards and looks at Undertaker's cocky grin. He suddenly pushes all his chips into the middle of the table. "Ok. I call," Liten says and flips over two pair, aces and jacks.

Undertaker lays down his cards. "Read 'em and weep son! Four kings!"

Liten groans and slams his head and paws to the table while Undertaker scoops up all the chips.

Safari Chip and the dogs laugh at the mouse. Then, Safari Chip makes his way to Maverick and Goose. The backups sit in front of a TV watching a hockey video game simulation. "Hey. You guys ready for the big game?"

"Yes sir," Goose assures.

"What are you playing?"

"Oh we're not playing. We're watching a game." Maverick holds out his hooves to show he has no controller.

"Which game?"

"IAHL Hockey," Maverick says.

"We're simulating a game to see who's going to win tonight," Goose explains.

"Who's winning?" Safari Chip asks.

Maverick and Goose look at each other uneasy.

"It's bad Chip," Goose says.

"How bad?" Safari Chip asks.

"10-0," Maverick says.

"Well it's a good thing that's just a video game. We'll show them tonight won't we?"

"Absolutely!" Maverick answers.

"For sure!" Goose agrees.

Safari Chip pats them on the back and walks to check on Sammie and Harlan. The pair of Gamblers sit outside Harlan's locker. "Guys?" Safari Chip says as he approaches.

"Hey Chip," Sammie says.

Harlan looks up. "Hi Chip."

"What's the secret meeting about?"

Sammie looks at Safari Chip with fear in his eyes. "No secret meeting. Just going over some game plans for tonight."

"Yeah. We just want to be as prepared as we can tonight," Harlan says.

In actuality, Sammie's teaching Harlan all the tricks the Gold Rush use to score on different goalies. The Gold Rush know he's telling Harlan their secrets though, and they plan to change up their style of play during tonight's game to confuse Harlan.

"That's good, but try to have a little bit of fun before we take the ice. I want you guys to be relaxed and have a good time tonight," Safari Chip orders.

Harlan nods. "Sure thing Chip."

"Will do," Sammie says.

"Have either of you guys seen Rodman?"

"I think he's in the video room." Harlan points to the door.

Safari Chip leaves the duo and heads for the video room. He passes Lovey. The teddy bear stands outside his locker, rocking out to an iPod and playing air guitar. Safari Chip gives him a high five as he passes.

Safari Chip cracks the door to the video room slightly and peeks inside. Except for the light provided by the TV, the room is totally dark. On the TV is an old Gamblers vs. Gold Rush game. Rodman intently watches, pauses, rewinds, and plays the footage again and again.

*

"Game time," Safari Chip yells.

The tummy of each and every one of the Gamblers jumps into his throat. Rodman leads his team running out of the locker room, down the dimly lit hallway, to the tunnel exit. They stop and wait in almost complete darkness. The tunnel and the arena lights are off except for a few strobe lights that roam the crowd. The arena announcer finishes the introductions of the Alaska Gold Rush to unruly and vehement boos.

The feeling in the tummies of the Gamblers turns from violent and tumultuous to eager and anxious. None of them can stand still.

Rodman looks around, just like he did the first night of his Gamblers career, trying to take in everything around him and hold on to every passing moment. The arena is packed, the crowd is boisterous, and he can see the Gold Rush skating around their net. He looks at the faces of the fans as the strobe lights light them up. He smells the air and takes in the frosty scent and chilly burn of the ice. He notices something he didn't notice that first night. The other Gamblers seem to be doing the same thing as him. Rodman rallies them together in a huddle as Safari Chip catches up to them. "Hey! Can I get one more 1-2-3 Gamblers?" Rodman throws his flipper into the middle of the huddle. Everyone else follows suit and they do their Gamblers cheer.

The lights come up enough to light up the tunnel exit.

The arena announcer booms. "And now for *your Las Vegas Gamblers!* Starting in goal, number twenty, *Harlan T. Turtle!*"

Harlan throws his goalie mask down and races out underneath a green spotlight to the crazy loud cheering of the crowd.

"Starting at left wing, number seventeen, *Liten Mus!*"

Liten races out of the tunnel. He waves to the crowd as he skates underneath his usual white spot light. He reaches Harlan and points out Alston in the front row.

Alston gives them a thumbs up.

"Starting at right wing, number sixteen, *Lovey Bara!*"

Underneath a tie-dyed spotlight, Lovey skates onto the ice as fast as his little cub legs will take him.

"Starting on defense, number thirteen, *Morty "Undertaker" Curtains!*"

Undertaker skates slowly and ominously under a purple spotlight to the boards in front of the Gold Rush bench.

The Gold Rush watch him stand in front of their bench for a solid five seconds. They talk smack to him and wave him off until suddenly, he throws his hands up and an explosion of fireworks blinds and deafens the arena. The Gold Rush players jump in terror, fall down on the bench, or take cover. The hearts of all of them skip a beat. The explosion blinds them so much that they don't even see Undertaker laugh at them and skate off.

"Also starting on defense, number ninety-nine, *Keith Kane!*"

Kane skates briskly onto the ice under a red spotlight. He makes his way to the Gold Rush bench the same as his partner in crime.

Not in the mood for anymore hijinx, the Gold Rush motion for him to go away.

Kane eyeballs them menacingly and throws his front paws into the air the same as Undertaker. The Gold Rush players shield their faces, close their eyes, cover their ears, and jump in anticipation of explosions but nothing happens. Kane laughs sinisterly at them. The Gold Rush ease up, and as they do, Kane drops his paws, bringing on another blinding and deafening explosion of fireworks overhead that sends the Gold Rush jumping, falling, and hiding once more.

"And starting at center, the captain, number seventy-three, *Rodman T. Penguin!*"

Rodman skates out under a white spotlight. He avoids the theatrics of Undertaker and Kane, but makes sure to point with intent towards the Gold Rush bench, in particular at Jason. His rival yells and points back at him, but Rodman can neither hear, nor does he care, what Jason has to say. He joins the Gamblers on their side of the ice.

The Gamblers followers hold up signs praising Rodman and wave Rodman dolls over their heads. The Chill go especially crazy, clapping, cheering, and waving at Rodman, though their seats are too far from the ice for him to see them.

"Also in tonight's game for the Gamblers are number twenty-six, *Maverick Limpright*, and number zero, *Bruce Goose*." The arena announcer pauses as Maverick and Goose make their way out of the tunnel. "And making his return…" he pauses again.

Wanting it to be a big surprise, the Gamblers haven't announced the return of Sammie to the press. The crowd has no clue who could be making his return. Their excitement grows.

Finally, the arena announcer lets them off the hook. "Number eighty-one, *Sammie Lou*."

Sammie skates onto the ice and plays to the crowd, shouting and waving. He stops at center ice and cups his big furry ears for the crowd as if to say that he can't hear them. Each time he does it, the crowd gets louder and louder until he finally smiles at them and acknowledges their excitement. He's so wrapped up in the moment that he forgets that in sixty minutes of hockey he's going to have helped in breaking the hearts of all the fans and his teammates. A wink from Jason puts that thought directly back into his head. He feels like the biggest jerk in the world.

The lights come up all the way and the announcer continues. "The Gamblers are lead by general manager and head coach *Safari Chip!*"

Safari Chip walks onto the ice wearing Gamblers colors. His suit is black with gold trim, and white buttons. He wears a red shirt with a black tie. Even his safari hat is white with a red ribbon outlined in black and gold. He heads for the Gamblers bench as the Gold Rush starters jump onto the ice.

Both teams do laps around their net as they wait for the start of the game.

The announcer booms again. "Ladies and gentlemen please rise and gentlemen please remove your caps in honor of tonight's presentation of our national anthem."

The players skate to their blue lines and take off their helmets. The crowd rises and the lights are dimmed again. Red, white, and blue spotlights rain down upon the players on the ice, and the National Anthem rings out from the speakers.

Rodman finds an American flag in the rafters. He puts his right flipper over his heart and stares at it. He remembers many times looking at the South African flag during the national anthem as a member of the Chill. Though he's always wanted to be in America, in the IAHL, he feels it's good to remember how he got here. He'll always hold a special spot in his heart for his days as a Chill.

The National Anthem ends, and the lights come up all the way. Both teams head to their bench to get last minute instructions. The Gamblers huddle in close.

Safari Chip leans into the huddle. "Go out there, play hard, play smart, play Gamblers hockey, and most importantly have a good time."

The Gamblers all high fives each other, and they break for center ice. Both teams take their positions. Jason, wearing Rodman's lucky scarf prominently around his neck, lines up across from Rodman for the faceoff.

Rodman notices the scarf straightaway. "I suppose by wearing my scarf you think you'd upset me. Get into my head and make me play poorly."

Jason chuckles snidely.

"Don't count on it. I'm a little bit tougher than that. And by the way, I double checked my stick. It's not broken, and we don't even allow Sleepytime Tea in our locker room."

"I don't know why you worked so hard to get here. You know you guys can't beat us," Jason antagonizes.

"Don't be so sure of the outcome," Rodman warns.

"It's going to be fun pounding you guys into oblivion tonight," Jason continues to antagonize.

The referee pokes his head into their conversation. "If you two tough guys are done jawing, it's time to drop the puck."

Still with the tough guy attitude Jason says, "Alright."

"Let's play," Rodman says excitedly and drops his head.

The referee drops the puck.

Chapter 13: Championship Game Period One

Jason wins the faceoff. He pokes the puck out to Metz, who takes it down the ice to the blue line and dumps it in. Lovey and Rapture race for the puck near the boards. The Gold Rush vulture reaches it first and starts a flurry of passes, sending it to Jason, who finds Packer open on the right side of the ice. Packer draws a couple of Gamblers to him and passes it across the ice to Metz, who winds up and takes a shot.

Harlan slides to his left and catches the puck in his glove, and quickly flips it to Lovey. Lovey skates alongside Liten past two defenders. They get to the other end of the ice and cross the blue line where only Metz and Iggy are there to defend. Both Gold Rush players skate towards Lovey leaving Liten completely uncovered.

Liten bangs his stick on the ice to get Lovey's attention. "Lovey! Here!"

Metz and Iggy crowd Lovey. The grizzly cub can only slightly see Liten through the intrusive opponents. He holds the puck patiently while the defenders converge upon him. At just the last moment, Lovey manages to eek the puck through Metz's legs. His patience does two things. It gets him bowled over by both Gold Rush players, but it also distracts Haas, and he doesn't see the pass.

Liten one times the puck past Haas into the net. The goal lights go off and the arena speakers play the slot machine jackpot noise.

The crowd goes bonkers.

The Gamblers go bonkers.

Rodman passes Jason and the rest of the Gold Rush players that joined the play too late. He jumps onto Liten for a big hug, knocking the tiny mouse down to the ice. "Alright Liten!"

The other Gamblers skate into the celebration. Hugs go round. Before going back to center ice for their next faceoff, they make a detour to their bench to high five the others. They continue their detour and make their way to Harlan for knuckle bashes.

Rodman skates into the faceoff grinning.

Jason snarls. "Smile while you can Rodman. Unless you guys can score about seven more, you have no chance."

"Blah, blah, blah. I see your beak moving, but all I hear is blah, blah, blah," Rodman shakes his head animatedly and uses his flipper to mimic a quacking beak.

Jason growls.

The referee drops the puck, and Rodman wins this time. Jason tries to push him after he loses the faceoff, but Rodman is quick to get out of the way, and Jason falls face first on the ice. Rodman gives him an extra push with his stick after he's fallen to keep him down.

Kane takes the puck down the ice, but an errant pass sends it to Iggy, and the play moves the other way. The Gamblers play man to man defense, but the Gold Rush get them tangled up them with their trademark of quick passes. Iggy passes the puck to Metz near the blue line. Metz passes it to Packer at the other end of the blue line. Packer passes it to Rapture on the wing, and Rapture sends it to Jason behind the net. With each pass, the Gamblers lose a little more ground on the player they're defending.

Iggy skates in front of the net, and Jason fakes a pass to him. Rodman buys the fake and leaves Jason to defend Iggy. This leaves Jason free to make a move the other way for a wrap around. Rodman realizes too late and tries to go back and fend Jason off, but Jason is already on the other side of the net completing his wrap around.

The goal lights go off.

The crowd boos.

The Gold Rush celebrate.

The Gamblers stomachs sink. The exhilaration they felt just moments ago with the lead dissipates and gives way to desperation.

Even Rodman wrestles with the idea that this feels like every other game they played against the Gold Rush this season. He sees the look of distress on his teammates and knows he can't let them stay down. He skates into the middle of them. "It's just one goal guys. The game's tied. It's a brand new game is all. We can still win this."

They acknowledge him with nods, but their faces say they're still rattled.

Rodman and Jason take their positions for another faceoff. They don't jabber this time.

The referee drops the puck.

Jason wins.

Packer grabs the puck and passes it to Iggy as he crosses the blue line. Iggy takes a shot on goal that is blocked by Harlan. The puck bounces to Jason, and he passes it back to Iggy. The iguana misplays the puck, and as he turns to find it, Undertaker skates in and smashes him against the glass. The hit incapacitates Iggy.

Kane snags the loose puck and heads down ice. The Gamblers go back on offense and take a series of shots. Haas stops everything that comes even remotely close to him. Kane, Undertaker, and Lovey each take several shots only to be denied over and over.

Lovey tries to pass the puck to Rodman, but it's intercepted by Jason. Play moves the other way again. Jason skates fast towards Harlan. He dekes left and right as he moves in on goal. Harlan comes out of the net a few feet in anticipation of the shot. Jason makes a move on Harlan and the turtle stumbles and falls down. Jason skates past him and scores an easy second goal. The Gold Rush celebrate their first lead of the game. Up by a goal, Jason feels he can antagonize Rodman again. He points boorishly towards him and snickers.

Down by a goal, the Gamblers go into all out panic mode. They've been down this road before, the one where the Gold Rush get a lead and then pile on the points. Rodman hopes his team can hold up for the rest of the period until he and Safari Chip can calm them down during intermission.

Both teams head to center ice where another faceoff takes place. Jason wins again. He drops a shoulder into Rodman, sending him onto his back. Rodman gets up fast and skates back to the play. The Gold Rush get a quick shot off before Rodman can get there, but luckily for the Gamblers, it's blocked by Harlan.

Harlan tries to flip the puck to Lovey but it's picked off by Rapture. Rodman sees Harlan in trouble and skates fast, coming up behind, and pokes the puck away from Rapture.

Liten snags the loose puck, and the Gamblers head the other way. Metz skates towards Liten with his teeth out. Kane and Undertaker are far away, but Liten catches a glimpse of Alston in the crowd. The lion holds up an encouraging fist. Liten's demeanor changes from scared to tough. He side steps Metz, and the cat flies into the glass. Metz hits so hard that he knocks himself temporarily out.

The Gamblers set up with Kane and Undertaker at the blue line, Lovey on the right side of the ice, and Rodman to the left, almost behind the net. Liten surveys his team. He makes eye contact with Rodman. They each furrow their eyebrows, letting the other know a play is developing. Rodman skates out from behind the net, and Liten tries to pass him a one-timer, but as the puck reaches Rodman, Jason checks him hard. The puck glides behind the net and winds up with Packer.

The cat takes the puck back to the Gold Rush side of the ice.

Rodman gets up and back into the play as Undertaker fights Packer and Rapture for the puck along the boards. Rodman joins the fight, shoving his stick into the tangled mess of sticks. He pulls Rapture's stick away from the puck with his own stick, freeing up enough room for Undertaker to grab it.

The Gamblers head back to their side of the ice. Undertaker shoots the puck to Rodman as they skate. Rodman skates around Metz as he nears the blue line, but he gets blindsided by Jason for the third time in the game. Jason flies off the ground and smashes Rodman hard with his elbow, making sure to drive it into Rodman's face. The hit is vicious and dirty, but none of the referees see it. Rodman falls down woozy and bruised. The feathers around his eye turn black and blue. For added injury, Jason knees Rodman in the face as he's slumped over.

The crowd boos vehemently. They want a penalty called but get none.

Kane barks at the referees as play continues and Rodman remains on the ice in pain. "Open your eyes ref! That hit he just put on Rodman is worse than any hit me or Undertaker ever levied."

"I didn't see anything," the referee barks back.

Understandably upset, Undertaker skates to Jason, spins him around and shoves him.

Jason knows better than to get into a fight. He got away with the dirty hit, and he doesn't want to end up in the penalty box. He laughs at Undertaker and goads him into a fight. He'll gladly take a punch to put the Gamblers on the penalty kill. Undertaker pushes Jason again, this time forcefully in the chest. Jason continues to laugh, so Undertaker tries to punch him, but Jason ducks out of the way.

The attempted fight is broken up, and whistles blow. Undertaker winds up with a two minute penalty for roughing. He's furious as he's skated to the penalty box.

"Oh yeah. Of course you see that, but you missed my boy get his head taken off you blind bat!" Undertaker yells at the referee, who happens to be a bat.

"Watch it Undertaker," the referee says.

"Watch it? You watch it. How do you think Rodman ended up on the ice unable to stand? You think he just blacked out suddenly? You watch it!" Undertaker yells.

The referee places Undertaker in the penalty box and lets him get away with a little more than he normally would because it's the championship game, and he knows he and the rest of the officiating crew blew the call Undertaker is barking about.

Still woozy, Rodman stands up. Liten and Lovey try to help him, but he shakes off their help. He skates to the bench, knowing he needs to sit out the remaining forty seconds of the period.

Sammie, waiting patiently, is positive he'll finally get his chance to get in the game. The old feeling of despicability weighs on him. He tries to shake the feeling and stands up to take the ice. To his surprise, Safari Chip sends Goose to replace Rodman. Sammie sits back down and watches more dirty play from the Gold Rush. He wonders why a team that is seemingly better needs to cheat to win a game that they're already winning. His head spins round and round from Rodman gingerly touching under his eye to the action on the ice where the Gamblers struggle on defense back to Rodman, who continues to feel his bruised eye gently with his flipper to Safari Chip, whose face is awash with distress. He hears the crowd boo. A flashing light coming from the corner of his eye draws his attention back to the ice where Rapture has just scored on an assist from Jason to put the Gold Rush up 3-1.

The Gamblers look more dejected than ever. Undertaker comes out of the penalty box. Rodman sighs heavily and lowers his head. Sammie joins him in his sigh.

After the goal, thirteen seconds remain in the period.

A faceoff takes place, and the Gamblers lose. Despite the little bit of time left in the period, the Gold Rush get a flurry of shots off before the final buzzer.

Somehow, Harlan is able to stop them all.

The Gamblers trudge off the ice out of breath. Their adoring fans stand and cheer despite their team going into the intermission down by two goals. Their support makes Rodman smile.

Inside the locker room, each Gambler takes a seat in front of his locker. The carefree attitudes that were in the room just an hour ago are gone, replaced by sullenness and fatigue.

Safari Chip stands in front of his team. "Ok guys. It's not over. In fact it's far from over."

"They're playing dirty Chip," Lovey interrupts.

"That's ok," Safari Chip assures them. "They always play dirty. We have to play smart because of that. The refs can't see everything out there. It's a travesty the way they didn't get a penalty for boarding Rodman. But look what happened. They got a power play when we retaliated, and now we're down by two goals instead of one because of that. Don't get caught up in their dirty tactics. They'll get called on those plays sooner or later. Play smart. Play Gamblers hockey. Watch out for each other, but don't get into fights. Check and check hard, but don't board. We can do this."

The team, Sammie included, yells in unison, letting their coach know they're with him.

"Alright! Now, grab a drink, tighten those skates, and do what it is you guys do during intermission. In about fourteen minutes, we have a hockey game to go win," Safari Chip yells.

The players yell excitedly again and go to put some fluids in their tummies.

Sammie, a train wreck of guilt and uneasiness, sneaks out into the hallway.

*

In the stands, the Chill wait out intermission, eating cotton candy, popcorn, and pizza.

Dolvy sips a drink from a blue and white striped cup. "Say uhhh, Jason's playing kind of dirty tonight. I don't remember him being that kind of a player."

"I do. I had to pull him into my office plenty of times. I always thought I could get him to improve his attitude, but I couldn't." The Coach shakes his head.

"He sure is hitting Rodman hard," Spoedige says.

"That's because he's jealous." Pikkewyn narrows his eyes at the thought.

*

Sammie walks far away from the Gamblers locker room. He looks over his shoulder a few times to make sure he's alone. He passes a set of doors and doesn't see Jason hiding off to the side. Jason hollers Sammie's name and startles him enough to make him literally jump.

"Don't do that," Sammie says.

"A little jumpy aren't you Sam?" Jason laughs.

Sammie shrugs.

"So I talked with some of the boys. We're going to get you in the game."

"How are you going to do that?"

"Let's just say that Mus may be skating onto the ice this period, but the only way he's getting off is on a stretcher."

Sammie's shaken up. He likes Liten. He doesn't want him to get hurt. "You guys are going to..."

"And when he comes off, they're going to put you on," Jason cuts him off.

"I know but..."

"What's the matter kid? You're not thinking about backing out are you?"

Sammie doesn't respond.

"You better not," Jason warns. His aggressive attitude doesn't help cheer Sammie up. Jason lightens his tone. "Look kid. Just think of this as an investment in your future. Next year at this time, you'll be a Gold Rush, but I've got to get back to my locker room."

Sammie still doesn't respond, and Jason heads off.

Chapter 14: Championship Game Period Two

A bevy of boos greet the Gold Rush as they skate back onto the ice. The teams switch sides. The lights come up.

The speakers blare. "And now, returning to the ice *your Las Vegas Gamblers!*"

The boos turn to cheers as Rodman leads the Gamblers out of the tunnel. He won a grand total of two faceoffs in the first period. He knows he's going to have to do better than that in the second period.

The players do laps around their new nets, and wait to be called to center ice for the period's first faceoff.

The referee signals for both teams to get into position.

"How'd you like the first period Rodman? Or can't you remember it after that last hit?" The pleasure that Jason derives out of physically punishing Rodman is creepy.

Rodman wonders if the IAHL has a no psycho policy and if he can get Jason tested for it. "It's far from over Jason."

"Well, in case you forgot, you guys have never scored more than three goals against us." He points to the scoreboard. "And, with the score being 3-1, that means you'll have to score at least four."

"We'll see what happens in the end," Rodman says.

"Yeah we will," Jason agrees with more than a tinge of arrogance.

Rodman has had enough of Jason's smack talk and bad mouthing. He changes his mind about winning the faceoff when the referee skates between them and holds the puck out. Instead, Rodman goes for straight for Jason, knocking him down.

The puck lands and remains unmoved until Liten skates in, takes it, and dumps the puck into the offensive zone. He races Metz and reaches the puck first, but he's met by a cross check from Packer when he attempts to move the puck. Another illegal move goes unnoticed by the referees but not the crowd. They boo loud and violently.

Packer pokes the puck to Rapture, who takes it over center ice and then the other blue line. The Gold Rush set up on offense. Rapture and Packer pass the puck back and forth a few times before Packer sees Iggy get loose from Lovey on the wing. He shoots the Marine Iguana the puck.

In front of the net, Jason and Rodman fight for position. Rodman tries to keep Jason out of the play while Jason tries to obstruct Harlan's view. Jason notices all three referees looking elsewhere and cross checks Rodman in the back. Rodman shakes it off. Jason cross checks him again. Rodman shakes it off again but turns to shove Jason off of him. As Rodman turns back to the play, Jason uses excessive force with his next cross check to knock Rodman down.

Iggy skates by the front of the net as Rodman falls down. He uses Rodman and Jason as blockers to take Harlan by surprise. He shoots around the traffic they create, through an open lane, and over Harlan's shoulder into the net. The goal puts the Gold Rush up 4-1.

The crowd boos ferociously.

The Gold Rush celebrate again.

The Gamblers move back to center ice looking like a team already defeated.

When the puck is dropped, Jason wins again. The Gold Rush take the puck over their blue line swiftly and effortlessly. Metz and Iggy each take a shot on goal, and Jason takes two.

One of the only Gamblers left showing some fight is Harlan, who stops all four shots. The Gamblers defense is sluggish. Undertaker and Kane play soft, not hitting players the way they normally do. Liten's rage for the cats is lacking. Most of the Gamblers look like they're saving themselves for the next game, though win or lose there will be no next game.

Jason takes a third shot. It's blocked by Harlan and collected by Kane, though he seems surprised to wind up with it. He quickly passes it ahead to Lovey. The Gamblers spring to life for a moment, and they all hustle back on offense. Lovey, Liten, and Rodman get a three on two scoring chance. As they move in on goal, Haas comes out of the net in anticipation of the shot. Lovey rears back and fakes a shot. Haas flinches at the fake shot, but Lovey kicks the puck with his skate Liten's way. Liten makes his way around Haas and taps that puck past him.

The Gamblers get back to within two goals. Liten pumps his fist and skates to the glass where Alston is sitting. The fans pound the glass at him, and Alston points to Liten with a loud growl. Liten gives him his best version of a growl back and pounds the glass with the other fans.

Suddenly, Alston's excited demeanor changes to horror.

Liten never sees Metz, but he feels his whole body crush under the weight of the cat as he gets boarded from behind. Liten's eyes close and his helmet leaves scratches on the glass as his head hits it and ricochets off. Fireworks erupt behind his eyelids, and pain shoots through every inch of his body. Before he can even collapse to the ice, Packer comes in and smashes him from the other side, causing him to pass out.

Alston growls threateningly at the Gold Rush cats and tries to climb the glass to get on the ice. It takes security and a few nearby fans to restrain him.

Whistles blow all over the place.

Most of the Gamblers were watching Liten celebrate with the crowd when Metz hit him. None were able to stop the wicked cat because they were taken by surprise. It isn't even until after the hit by Packer that any of them have a chance to make a move towards Liten.

Undertaker and Kane reach their fallen comrade first and violently throw the cats to the ice. Rodman dives on top of Liten, covering him from further injury. Players from both benches jump onto the ice, joining the mob scene. Sammie even skates out to help Rodman protect Liten. He looks on in horror at his bruised, beaten, and unconscious buddy. It almost makes him throw up knowing he did nothing to stop this. Safari Chip and Coil exchange heated words from their benches.

It takes the referees over five minutes to get everyone separated. Once the players from both teams are separated, the referees convene to go over what penalties to levy to which players. They give Undertaker and Kane leeway for throwing the cats to the ice, considering the severity of the hit on their teammate who is still being attended to by Gamblers personnel.

The head referee goes to the scorer's table and announces the penalties to them while the other referees skate Metz and Packer off the ice to overwhelming cheers from the crowd.

The arena announcer broadcasts the penalties. "Number thirty-one. Alaska. Five minutes for boarding and ten minute game misconduct. Number twelve. Alaska. Five minutes for boarding and ten minute game misconduct with a match penalty assessed to both for intent to injure."

The cats don't seem at all concerned with their penalties. They smile upon the lifeless Liten as the referees skate them past the mouse on their way off the ice.

"Nice goal Mus!" Metz cracks whip as he passes.

"Yeah. Good luck getting up mouse!" Packer calls psychotically.

The head referee pulls Rodman and Jason aside. He warns both that any retaliation or further dirty play will result in more players being thrown out or possible forfeiture of the game.

"Sure. They get to injure, maim, and knock us around, but if we try to protect ourselves, you're going to call it retaliation. Why don't you try calling it down the middle?" Rodman loses his cool with the referee.

"Why don't you stop whining?" Jason goads.

Rodman tries to get at Jason, but the referees step between them and keep them separated.

On the ice, Liten finally stirs. He opens his eyes, but he can barely remember what happened, where he is, or what's going on. The team doctor determines he's ok to move, but Liten needs the assistance of Undertaker and Kane to stand and skate off the ice to the tunnel where he'll go to the locker room to be further evaluated.

The crowd gives Liten a standing ovation.

On the bench, Safari Chip calls to Sammie. "Ok kid, you're in."

Sammie grabs his stick and jumps onto the ice purposefully. He skates to the side of Rodman at center ice for the next faceoff. He nods at Rodman, and Rodman nods back. The Gamblers prepare to start their power play.

"Five on three for five whole minutes, and it doesn't matter how many times we score. It's going to be five on three the whole time," Rodman antagonizes.

"Shut up Hott Rod. Oh, except you're not that hot, are you? In fact, you've been pretty ice cold tonight. No goals, no assists. Have you even taken a shot? I mean, other than the five or six shots to the head you've taken from me."

"Talk all you want Jason. You know in the next five minutes we're at least going to tie this game."

The referee drops the puck, and Rodman wins. He shoots the puck back to Undertaker, and Undertaker takes the puck down the ice. Near the blue line, Undertaker passes it back to Rodman, who dumps it into the zone.

Lovey and Rapture race for the puck. Rapture gets his stick on it before Lovey, but he Kane comes into the play from the other direction and lights the vulture up with a devastating hit, taking the wounded bird out of the play.

Lovey grabs the loose puck and finds Rodman skating away from Iggy. Lovey shoots him a pass. Rodman corrals the puck just as Undertaker sets up a pick on Iggy, causing him to fall down and be taken out of the play as well.

Rodman has Lovey to his left, Sammie to his right, and only Jason in front of him to defend all three Gamblers attackers.

Jason skates like a bulldozer towards Rodman.

Rodman has to decide quickly to pass the puck to either Lovey or Sammie. Either player is likely to score an easy goal. Ultimately, Rodman shoots the puck to Sammie, and Sammie doesn't hesitate. He slaps a shot at Haas so hard that it drops the hare on his back much the same way Harlan used to end up on his shell in the earlier parts of the season. The puck flies into the net with such force that it tears through the rope and leaves a hole in the net.

The goal lights go off.

The referees check out the hole in the netting in awe.

At 4-3, the Gold Rush lead is down to one.

Jason can't believe he's been double crossed. He's irate watching Sammie celebrate with the Gamblers.

Sammie looks Jason's way, makes eye contact, and snarls at him. He knows what Jason and the Gold Rush are capable of doing to their enemies, but as scary as that is, he doesn't want to be any part of their nefarious plan. He's made his choice, and he's chosen to help the Gamblers win it all. From what he's seen tonight, the Gold Rush might not be the best team after all. They're just bullies and cheats, and the Gamblers have done just fine to this point playing a clean game.

The teams head for their benches while the referees get new netting for the net. Jason bumps shoulders with Sammie threateningly on the way.

Once play is ready to resume, Jason takes his sweet time getting to center ice for the next faceoff.

Rodman greets Jason with a devious smile. "I told you we were going to tie this thing."

"You haven't tied anything," Jason grumbles.

"But I did get an assist. Not so cold anymore. And what did that take?" Rodman looks up to the scoreboard. "Sixteen seconds. We still have over four and a half minutes of power play."

The referee drops the puck, and Rodman wins again. He gets the puck out to Kane, who tries to pass it to Sammie, but his stick breaks when it hits the puck, and he has to race to the bench for a new one.

The puck essentially dies on the ice and is scooped up by Rapture. The vulture takes the puck all the way behind his own net to kill some time. With Gamblers approaching him from either side, Rapture clears the puck all the way down to the other side of the ice, killing more time.

Harlan skates out and passes the puck to Rodman so the Gamblers can go right back on the attack.

Back in their offensive zone, Rodman makes a move on Jason like he's going to the net. In one motion, he fakes a shot by rearing back his stick and pretending to fire the puck, but as he rears back, he actually hits the puck lightly behind him to Kane.

Jason dives to stop Rodman's shot with his body.

Kane moves around Rodman and Jason and blasts a shot.

Haas doesn't even have time to panic. He never sees the puck. Fortunately for him, Kane's shot ricochets off his chest protector. Unfortunately for him, the puck bounces to Lovey, and he fires a shot past the unsteady hare that ties the game at 4-4.

The arena goes nuts. They wave black, white, and red towels in circles. Some hold their Rodman dolls over their heads and shake them violently. The Chill jump up and down, spilling their food all over the place, on themselves, on the floor, and on other fans, none of whom seem to care. Alston growls triumphantly.

The Gamblers mob Lovey with hugs, pinning him against the glass as fans pound cheerfully at them. The celebration gets so rowdy that they fall to the ice and Lovey lies at the bottom of a five animal pile up. The Gold Rush scowl at the celebration.

The Gamblers get up and head to their bench for high fives and knuckle bashes. They make a detour to Harlan again before they head back to center ice for the next faceoff.

Jason doesn't say a word during the next faceoff and neither does Rodman.

The rest of the power play doesn't go as easily for the Gamblers as the first minute. The Gold Rush fight feverishly and effectively to kill off the rest of the penalty. The Gamblers get plenty of shots off, nineteen in all during the power play, but Haas is able to fend off seventeen.

When the penalties expire, the Gold Rush players that served the penalties, Conrad Brooks a goat, and Milky Cabrera, a white leopard come out of the box.

The game turns into a defensive battle in the final minutes of the period. Both teams struggle to set up on offense. Time and again they dump the puck in only to lose it to the other team. When they are able to get the puck into their offensive zone and maintain control of it, they make bad passes, take bad shots, have their sticks bumped, or have the puck stolen.

With thirty seconds left in the period, Jason gets a slight breakaway.

Rodman skates after him. He sees Harlan come out of the net. Rather than let Jason get a hat trick and an easy goal, Rodman wraps the curved end of his stick around Jason and hooks him.

Jason's sent spinning out of control. He falls, slides, and hits the boards hard. He grabs his flipper and winces in pain as he stands up.

A whistle blows, and Rodman gets a two minute hooking penalty. He knows there's a good chance the Gold Rush will score while he's in the penalty box, but if he didn't hook Jason, he probably would have scored for sure.

The pain in Jason's shoulder fades as he takes his spot in the faceoff circle on the power play. He lines up across from Sammie. He creases his eyebrows at Sammie. "What's your problem? You're supposed to be helping us."

"I changed my mind," Sammie grunts.

"Don't you want to be a winner? A Gold Rush?"

"I do want to be a winner Jason, but I want to be a Gambler. These guys have worked too hard to get here to be cheated out of their chance. They put their trust in me, and I'm not going to let them down."

"You'll pay for this Lou! No one turns their back on us. There's still one period left, and you better watch yourself. 'Cause what we're going to do to you will make what happened to Liten look like a minor bump on the head."

Sammie doesn't like being threatened and growls at Jason.

The referee skates in and drops the puck. Sammie wins the faceoff, but Jason runs him over.

The Gamblers try to hold the puck in their zone for as long as they can to kill some clock before they clear it. Packer intercepts the clearing attempt, and the Gold Rush are able to remain onside.

A pass from Packer goes to Jason, and he takes a very quick and accurate shot on goal.

Harlan, looking more like a hare than a turtle, jumps in front of the puck and whacks it away with his glove. The puck bounces out to Rapture, who shoots at the empty side of the net and Harlan makes another stop, this time diving to flick the puck away with his stick. Jason rushes to collect the rebound. He shoots over the sprawled out Harlan, and Harlan makes a third miracle save by kicking the puck with his leg pads while on his shell.

Undertaker, Kane, and Lovey fight to clear the puck away from Harlan, but they can't get their sticks on it.

Harlan's luck runs out as the puck goes right back to Jason, who not only shoots and scores, but gets his hat trick. Jason's third goal of the game puts the Gold Rush back on top. The score is 5-4 with only three seconds left to go in the period.

Rodman comes out of the penalty box. He and Jason complete a meaningless faceoff and time expires with the two penguins pushing and shoving one another. Once their respective teams separate and contain their angry penguin, the Gamblers rush excitedly to their locker room to overwhelming cheers from their fans.

*

The Gamblers walk into the locker room with some pep in their step. No one sits. They all stand in a close nit group in front of Safari Chip. "Great period of hockey guys. We come in here down, but we're down by only one this time. We've still got twenty minutes to play. Twenty minutes left in our season, win or lose. This is the best game of hockey I've ever seen you guys play. So let's get back out there and cap it off with a win, because you guys deserve it."

The Gamblers shout incoherently and joyously.

"Everyone huddle up," Safari Chip says.

Everyone except Sammie huddles around him and puts their hands, flippers, wings, hooves, and paws into the huddle.

"Come on Sam. Get in here." Safari Chip waves to his winger.

Sammie hesitates. He looks like a koala bear whose favorite eucalyptus leaves just went extinct. "I have to tell you guys something."

"What's up?" Undertaker asks.

Everyone can tell something is weighing on Sammie's mind.

Sammie hesitates. "When I came back to the team, I didn't have any intentions of helping you guys win the championship."

"What do you mean?" Kane asks.

"Yes. What are you talking about?" Liten asks.

"When I was here, this was a really bad team. Then, when I left, you guys started winning. I saw how everyone at the Mardi Gras Room followed your games with such enthusiasm and excitement, and it made me jealous. So one night Jason offered me a contract with the Gold Rush if I'd help him sabotage you guys, and I agreed."

Safari Chip and his team look at Sammie mortified, angry, dismayed, and disgusted as they continue holding their circle.

There's a long tense stare down between the Gamblers and Sammie.

Something about the look on Sammie's face and something about the way he played in the last period alerts Safari Chip to the fact that Sammie hasn't been going along with the plan. The rest of the team might not see it or even care to try, but he tries to help Sammie out. "But you scored a goal for us."

"That's right. Why would you do that if you're helping the Gold Rush?" Lovey, ironically the most hesitant to accept Sammie back, is the quickest to help bail him out.

"That's just it. I can't do it. I look at the camaraderie around this room, and I think back to how you gave me a second chance, and I can't sabotage you guys. Now, I have to ask for a third chance. I know I have two strikes, but I promise if you can trust me one last time, I won't strikeout." Sammie crosses his heart with a finger.

The Gamblers looks around at one another. No one knows what to say. No one smiles. No one gives Sammie any indication of anything. Their emotions are a whirlwind of betrayal, anger, pity, and friendship all at once.

Sammie's sure he's screwed up his days as a Gambler.

The tension in the room is thick, and though the silence lingers for only a few seconds, it seems like days.

Just as he's about to turn and head out of the locker room, Sammie catches a glimpse of Rodman smiling at him. His ears perk up. Lovey smiles at him too. Then, Safari Chip smiles and slowly, one by one, all the Gamblers smile in his direction. They motion for him to join them in the circle. Sammie runs to join them, wearing the biggest smile any Gambler has worn all season. He throws his paw into the mix.

"One, two, three, Gamblers!"

Chapter 15: Championship Game Period Three

The Gamblers, led by Sammie, skate onto the ice for the third period.

Jason watches them charge out of the tunnel with contempt. He's set his mind to do two things. The first thing is to do whatever it takes to help his team survive the final twenty minutes of regulation. The second is to injure as many Gamblers as possible before the game ends.

The teams switch sides again and line up for the period's first faceoff.

The referee positions himself between the two penguins, expecting to hear the heated banter that has been going on all game. To his surprise, neither captain jaws at the other. He does a quick double take to make sure he's seeing right and then drops the puck.

Rodman swipes a little harder and a little quicker at the puck and wins the faceoff.

Not many words are exchanged during the third period. Both teams let their actions do the talking. The pace is fast and furious.

The Gamblers cross the blue line with the puck and get it to Rodman. He takes a shot on goal, but it's blocked.

To the other end of the ice goes the play. The Gold Rush set up and get a pass to Jason. He takes a shot on goal, but it too is blocked.

The scoreboard shows 18:19 to go in the game. The score remains 5-4.

Sammie gets smashed hard against the glass by Jason. He falls to the ice and has a hard time getting up, but he makes it to the bench and Liten, bandaged but ok, takes his place.

Rapture races down the ice with the puck. Kane meets him near the blue line and lays a clean hit on him, knocking the bird off his feet.

Rodman grabs the loose puck and is immediately met by a stick to the face from Jason.

Two referees blow their whistles.

Jason gets a high sticking penalty and goes to the penalty box.

With 16:35 to go in the game, the Gamblers start their power play.

They lose the first faceoff and struggle to gain control of the puck. Eventually, they force the Gold Rush to clear the puck, and they are able to get it. When they finally set up in their zone, they only get a couple of shots off. Kane blasts a shot from near the blue line that is caught in Haas' glove, and Lovey takes a bad shot it traffic. Though it wasn't a good shot, it was worth a try as nothing else ever developed and the power play was running out.

Jason comes out of the penalty box with 14:35 to go in the game and the score still at 5-4.

The Gold Rush gain control and go back on the attack. Iggy takes a shot. Harlan blocks it with his glove, and it flips over and behind the net. Conrad, Undertaker, and Lovey fight for the loose puck. Lovey frees the puck and sends it out to Liten.

Liten snags it and skates back towards Haas. Milky skates at him with his teeth unveiled and threatening. Liten can't believe these cats won't learn. He skates right at the snarling cat and knocks him down to the delight of the crowd. The puck skids away a bit, but Liten regains control of it and continues down the ice with Rodman. As they near the blue line, Rodman crosses before the puck, and play is stopped on an offsides call.

After a faceoff, the Gamblers settle in on offense and hold the puck in their zone for a long time. Still, they can't break through Haas' superb goaltending. They even try to switch things up by sending out Maverick and Goose, two of the freshest players, for the injured Liten and tired Lovey. Even that doesn't work.

Eventually, the Gold Rush regain control of the puck, and Maverick and Goose rush to the bench, allowing Sammie and Lovey to get back on the ice.

Before the two Gamblers can skate into the play, Jason passes the puck past Rodman to Iggy. He passes it right back to

Jason. The quick passing draws Harlan to the wrong side of the net, and Jason shoots. He smiles his repulsive smile, knowing he's about to put the Gold Rush up 6-4, essentially ending the game.

Out of nowhere, Rodman slides on his belly in front of the empty side of the net. The puck goes over him, but he reaches his stick up just in the nick of time to deflect it away.

Jason's nasty smile turns to exasperation. He skates with malice towards Rodman, who is defenseless on his belly. His intent is to pummel and incapacitate Rodman, but just before he reaches Rodman, Undertaker skates in and demolishes Jason. The hit isn't exactly clean, but the referees have their sights on the action heading in the other direction.

The scoreboard shows 12:56 left in the game. The score remains 5-4.

Rodman skates into the play and gets a stealthy pass from Sammie. He tries a wrap around behind the net but is denied. Haas blocks the puck with his leg pads and covers it up with his glove.

A referee blows his whistle and play stops.

Jason skates to the dead play still seething about his blocked shot and getting pushed around. Like the goon he is, he skates up to Rodman and pushes him in the face. Rodman pushes him back. It takes the referees and both teams to separate the penguins. Neither team wants to be without their best player for the final minutes.

The game starts back up, and for a while it looks more like a UFC fight than a hockey game. Both teams are tired of being hit, and one by one everyone starts retaliating. Liten smashes Rapture and Milky against the glass repeatedly, eventually putting the vulture and white tiger on the run any time he's in the area. Undertaker and Kane trade blows with Conrad and Iggy. Jason hits Rodman, Sammie, Lovey, and Liten as often as he can. His hits take a toll of them, especially Liten. Rodman makes sure to hit Jason a bunch too. Maverick and Goose sub in for the other Gamblers here and there and levy some hits of their own on the Gold Rush. At one point, Jason and Rapture try to take Liten out of the game for good by smashing him at the same time from either side, but Liten sidesteps them, and sends them crashing into each other. The Gold Rush take a timeout to give their captain and alternate a moment to rest.

The Gamblers skate to their bench and are met by a very angry Safari Chip. "What the heck are you guys doing out there? Are you trying to tie this thing up or are you trying to get the attention of MMA scouts?"

No one responds. They know he's right. With only 8:01 left in the game, and them trailing by one, they're wasting time.

"When this thing resumes, I want you guys to go out there and really hurt the Gold Rush. Hit them where it'll hurt them the most... the scoreboard."

"Yeah!" they all scream in unison.

The timeout ends. Both teams head to center ice. Jason wins the faceoff, and the Gold Rush go out on offense.

The puck is taken over the blue line by Milky, though he nearly loses it to some crafty defense by Undertaker. At the last second, Milky is able to poke it to Rapture.

In front of the net, Jason and Rodman fight for position. Obstructed by the dueling penguins, Harlan fights to see the play. Jason skates behind Rodman and cross checks him in the back repeatedly. When Rodman won't fall, Jason uses his stick and hits him in the back of the neck.

Rodman falls to the ice in as much pain as he's been in all night. He gets up slowly and bumps chests with Jason. He remembers Safari Chip's warning to not fight and skates away from his nemesis to defend the play.

Iggy takes a shot and it's deflected up into the crowd by Kane. Play stops.

Rodman lines up across from Jason for another faceoff with 7:25 left. Both penguins are tired, sore, and out of breath as they wait for the puck to be dropped.

"Why don't you give it up Rodman? Before you get seriously hurt," Jason pants.

"Why don't you just shut up? I've said it before and I'm saying it again. All I ever hear from you is blah, blah..."

A wad of spit from Jason's beak interrupts Rodman. It lands on the protective glass that covers Rodman's eyes on his helmet. The look on Rodman's face looks as though Jason had thrown a sword his way rather than spit. Everything around Rodman fades. The crowd, his teammates, and the ice all blur. Even sound goes away. Jason remains in his sights however, and Rodman drops his stick and his gloves and leaps at Jason.

The referees back up and let the fight go on. They know that if they don't let them have it out this way that one of them likely won't be able to walk out of the arena by the time it's over.

Rodman throws a haymaker at Jason, but Jason ducks out of the way. They tango for a moment trying to land punches on the other. They continue to miss with their swings and Rodman slips and falls into Jason. They lock up and ever the dirty player, Jason tries to pull Rodman's jersey over his head so he can't see.

Rodman let's him pull and uses his own momentum in the other direction to jump out of the jersey. The move catches Jason off guard and causes him to stumble backwards. Rodman literally runs, on his skates, at Jason and spear tackles him to the ice. He unloads a flurry of punches that Jason can't defend. Jason is forced to endure the beating brought on by his own dumb actions.

With two good clean shots to the beak Rodman has Jason dazed as he lies on his prissy little tail. Rodman takes the opportunity to remove his scarf from Jason's neck. The referees step between the penguins and attempt to haul them both to the penalty box, but Rodman takes his scarf around the ice for a victory lap. The referees give chase as he skates around waving his scarf to the cheering fans. After a full lap and a half, Rodman stops to put the scarf around his own neck where it rightfully belongs. It's only then that two referees grab him by the flippers and drag him to the penalty box to an overwhelming endorsement by the crowd. The Chill and Alston go especially crazy.

Both penguins get five minute penalties for fighting. The scoreboard still shows 7:25 left in the game. The score remains 5-4. But now, the Gamblers will be without Rodman until 2:25 to go in the game. That's a much bigger factor in the outcome for them, down by one, than it is for the Gold Rush.

Play resumes four on four. The Gamblers send out Sammie, Lovey, Undertaker, and Kane. The Gold Rush send out Rapture, Iggy, Milky, and Conrad.

For most of the next five minutes, the period continues much the same way as is has to this point. A defensive battle with great goaltending ensues. Sammie takes a shot on goal and is denied. Undertaker and Kane also take shots on goal that are denied. In the opposite direction, Harlan makes spectacular stops on three different shots from Rapture. The vulture grows more and more frustrated with each miss.

The scoreboard shows 3:33 left in the period. The score remains 5-4.

Rodman and Jason yell at each other in the penalty box.

Sammie wins a faceoff against Iggy.

Hass blocks two more shots.

Harlan blocks two more shots.

Lovey dives and uses his body to block a shot. The puck bounces to Kane, and the Gamblers go back on the attack. They aren't desperate yet, but their window is closing.

The score board shows 2:25 left in the third period. The score remains 5-4.

Rodman and Jason come out of the penalty box. Caught off guard by the oncoming play, Jason is immediately checked by Sammie, who has been watching the time on the penalty expire and has been waiting near the penalty box for just that reason.

Lovey passes the puck to Rodman, and he passes it to Undertaker. The Lhasa Apso shoots but is denied. Haas uses his stick to drop the puck from the air and passes it to Jason, who skates fast and hard towards Harlan on a breakaway.

Rodman skates even faster to catch up to Jason. He uses his stick to disrupt Jason's control, and the puck squibs out and goes behind the net.

The scoreboard shows 1:09 left in the game. The score remains 5-4.

Rodman recovers the puck and takes off towards Haas. He weaves in between and past defenders on his way down the ice.

Jason follows two strides behind. He senses trouble, as Rodman moves in on Haas.

Rodman sees the perfect spot to sink the puck. He slows down just enough to get into perfect position and rears his stick back.

Jason drops his own stick and catches up to Rodman just in time to grab Rodman's stick and pull it completely from his grasp.

Rodman and everyone else in the arena stop and look on in shock at the crazy-eyed maniac penguin.

Jason throws Rodman's stick across the ice.

Whistles blow all over the place.

Jason does little more than stand huffing and puffing in front of Rodman with a look of defeat scribbled all over his face. Two referees skate to Jason and grab him by his flippers. The crowd wants a penalty shot, but Jason is given an interference penalty instead and he's forced to finish out the game in the penalty box.

Rodman skates to the third referee. "Hey, we need to call our timeout."

The referee announces the timeout to the scorer's table.

The Gamblers skate to their bench, and the Gold Rush do likewise. Rodman motions for Harlan to come to the bench too.

"Come into the bench Harlan." Rodman motions to his goalie.

"Into the bench?" Harlan asks.

"What's on your mind Rodman?" Safari Chip asks.

"I have a plan," Rodman assures his team. "Everyone huddle up close."

The Gamblers huddle around Rodman and Harlan, and those two disappear into the middle of the huddle.

After their minute is up, a whistle blows and a referee shouts to both benches, "Time's up. Let's go guys."

The Gamblers take the ice on a five on four power play. Their five skates include Undertaker, Kane, Lovey, Sammie, and Liten. Rodman is conspicuously absent.

In the stands, Spoedige asks aloud to anyone listening, "Where's Rodman?"

"What?" Dolvy asks. He and the rest of the guys look to the ice.

"He's not out there," Spoedige swears.

"No way," Pikkewyn says, still looking for Rodman.

Sure enough there's no Rodman on the ice.

"Why wouldn't they have their best player on the ice during a power play in the final sixty-two seconds of the championship game that they are currently losing by one goal?" Dolvy asks.

The Coach smiles a huge smile. "Oh boy. Just you guys watch. I know what they're thinking."

The Chill wish they knew what was going on, but they focus in on the play like The Coach tells them to.

Sammie lines up across from Iggy for the faceoff. Even Iggy looks confused by Rodman's absence. He gives Sammie a questioning look. Sammie gives him no indication of what's going on.

The referee skates in and drops the puck.

Iggy wins the faceoff, getting the puck to Rapture, who passes it to Conrad. The outnumbered Gold Rush run as much time off the clock as they can before blasting the puck down the ice, clearing it.

Harlan goes behind the net and gathers the puck for Sammie. Sammie goes behind the net, seizes it, and holds it while the Gamblers get into position. Once everyone is in the appropriate spot, Sammie makes a fast break for the other end of the ice with his teammates around him.

Five on four they race as the final forty seconds tick away.

Near the blue line, Sammie passes it to Lovey. Lovey takes it across into the zone, but he's immediately met and pressured by Conrad. He's forced to dump the puck behind the net.

Liten races to the loose puck and is able to get it. He passes it to Kane without difficulty, though Rapture races towards him like a speeding freight train. Rapture skates so hard at Liten that when Liten sidesteps the oncoming vulture, Rapture crashes into the glass hard, injuring his right wing. He falls down and clutches his injured limb, rendering the game five on three momentarily.

Kane and Undertaker pass the puck back and forth across the blue line a few times, trying to draw their opponents away from the net so they can get an open shot. While they pass the puck around, Rapture gets up and skates slowly to the bench looking for P.J. Hood, a rhino and the final player on the Gold Rush bench, to take his place.

On the other end of the ice, with twenty-five seconds to go, Harlan skates out of his net and down the ice as if he's going to join the play. The crowd is astonished at the sight.

Rapture is too. He's so astonished at the odd scene of the goalie passing him that it causes him to freeze in his tracks, keeping his replacement off the ice.

Harlan reaches center ice before the other players start to notice him. He looks to Jason and winks at him as he passes the penalty box.

Inside the penalty box, Jason flips out. He knows what's going on and he yells a warning to his teammates, but they can't hear him above the roar of the crowd.

As Harlan approaches the blue line, the other players on the ice start to notice him. Most of the Gold Rush are so confused they lose focus.

Harlan drops his gloves and keeps coming.

All in the arena, except the extremely focused Gamblers players, look at Harlan disorientated. The confusion felt by everyone peaks when he takes off his goalie's mask to reveal that he isn't Harlan at all, but rather Rodman in Harlan's gear and jersey. Rodman throws the goalie mask to the ice.

Twenty seconds to go.

Rodman skates by and takes the puck from Undertaker.

Conrad is the first Gold Rush player to snap out of his confused state. He tries to skate away from Undertaker, but Undertaker blocks him out of the play.

On the other side of the blue line, Kane blocks Milky from the play.

Rapture reaches the bench, and P.J. jumps onto the ice.

With P.J. behind the play, and Milky and Conrad being blocked out, Iggy is the sole defender against Rodman, Sammie, Liten, and Lovey.

P.J. skates urgently for Rodman, but he's checked roughly by Lovey and lands on his back.

Seventeen seconds to go.

Iggy stands his ground in front of Haas, trying to help fend off the approaching penguin, but Sammie skates in front of Iggy, obstructing not only his view, but and Haas' view as well. Liten further blocks their view by skating between Iggy and Haas, adding to their confusion.

Rodman wraps around the net.

Fifteen seconds to go.

Haas slides in Rodman's direction in anticipation of the shot.

Sammie and Liten continue to block Iggy.

Rodman hits the breaks and wraps back around the other way.

Haas can't get to his feet as quick as he would like and loses sight of Rodman. He dives backwards and falls on his back as Rodman hits the breaks and wraps back around the other way again.

This time, Rodman finishes his wrap around, poking the puck just under Haas' skates, into the net.

Goal lights go off.

The Gamblers fans come unglued, flying out of their seats to cheer.

Rodman rushes away from the net, stumbling in Harlan's gear, as he skates to no particular destination. His teammates chase him, trying to catch and tackle him in celebration. They only catch him because he falls to his belly. Undertaker, Kane, Liten, Lovey, and Sammie dog pile on top of him.

Nine seconds remain on the clock.

On the Gamblers bench, Harlan pops up from the floor where he's been hiding in Rodman's jersey. He high fives Maverick and Goose. Then, all three of them turn to the fans behind the bench and high five them through the glass.

The door to the penalty box is stuck, and Jason can't get out. He yells at the penalty box attendant, but the door won't budge. He continues to yell at the attendant incessantly and doesn't notice the celebration on the ice make its way to him. The Gamblers, lead by Rodman, each tap the glass near Jason's face with their stick. The tapping takes him by surprise and startles him. The smiling and laughing faces of his opponents infuriate him. He screeches and pounds the penalty box glass with his flippers.

One of the referees helps pry the penalty box door open. The other referees try to round up the Gamblers for the next faceoff, but they aren't being cooperative. They skate to their bench and high five the rest of the team and continue to play to the crowd.

The penalty box door finally opens and Jason is freed. He attempts to skate to Rodman and the celebrating Gamblers as they do their laps, riling up the crowd. His intent is to hurt Rodman, but the other Gold Rush players see the anger all over his face and restrain him. They know they're going to need their volatile captain in overtime.

The referees finally get the Gamblers to stop horsing around and come to center ice with the threat of a delay of game penalty. Rodman is forced to finish out regulation as the goal tender since they already used their timeout and he doesn't have time to switch gear with Harlan. Sammie, still teeming with confidence and momentum, takes and wins the faceoff against Iggy.

Jason rides the bench, because Coil wants his hot-headed penguin to calm down before overtime starts.

The Gamblers set up in their offensive zone with four seconds left. With time left and an open shot, in an attempt to win the game, Kane blasts a shot, but it's blocked by Haas. Miraculously, Liten gets the rebound and has time to shoot. He too is denied. Haas covers up the puck, and regulation ends, though the Gamblers continue to try and score while the Gold Rush push at them and fight to keep the puck away.

While the fighting in front of the Gold Rush net goes on, Rodman races to the bench so he and Harlan can get into their own uniforms.

Overhead the arena announcer can barely be heard over the roar of the raucous crowd. "At the end of regulation the score is Las Vegas 5. Alaska 5. We're heading to overtime! After a one minute intermission, the game will resume in sudden death overtime. The first team to score a goal will become the IAHL Anderson Cup Champions!"

Safari Chip gives his players some last minute words of encouragement. "Ok guys, no matter what happens you're already winners." He wants to cover all the bases in case of a win or a loss. Then he adds, "But let's win this thing anyway!"

The festive pandemonium that comes from their bench is typical of the Gamblers.

Rodman and Harlan finish changing back into their gear just as the referee blows his whistle to start overtime.

The Gold Rush make their way slowly to center ice. They rarely struggle this bad and never against the Gamblers. They don't know what to make of their current predicament. All the momentum seems to be with the Gamblers.

Jason is one of their few players who remains arrogant, skating with a swagger as though the Gold Rush have already won.

There is no talk between Rodman and Jason as they faceoff. The referee drops the puck. Jason steals back some of the momentum with a win. He passes the puck to Milky, and he taps it over the blue line.

Rapture chases the puck down and blasts a quick shot.

Harlan drops to his knees and stops the puck between the padding on his legs. He holds the puck there with many of the Gold Rush players in front of him, trying to find the puck and poke it in the net. In a desperate attempt to push the puck through, the Gold Rush fall on top of Harlan and push him into the net.

The Gamblers fall on top of the Gold Rush, trying to get them off Harlan.

Whistles blow and play stops. Pushing and shoving follows as Gamblers and Gold Rush players pick each other out of the pile. No penalties are levied. Someone is going to have to commit a crime before the referees throw anyone in the penalty box now.

After the skirmish, another faceoff takes place. Jason wins again. Iggy passes the puck to Rapture. He then aims a shot at Harlan and draws him to that side of the net. Instead of shooting, Rapture passes the puck out to Jason on the other side of the net. Jason hesitates for a fraction of a second, smiles wickedly, double pumps, and one times the puck at the empty side of the net. He knows he's got a fourth goal and more importantly the game winner.

Once again, out of nowhere, Rodman dives at the shot. He throws his stick out in front of himself, keeping his eye on the puck the entire time, and with a combination of much skill and even more luck, he's able to knock the shot down. It drops right in front of Rodman as he lands with a thud. Despite having the wind knocked out of him, he's able to muster enough strength to flick the puck out to Kane.

Kane turns with the puck to head down the ice while Rodman gets up gingerly. The dog doesn't even complete his turn though because Rapture comes in and demolishes him so hard that both players fall to the ice.

Undertaker swoops in and collects the loose puck. Jason skates at him furiously. Undertaker sees him coming and ducks down. Instead of knocking Undertaker out of the play, Jason does a sunset flip over the dog. Undertaker skates hard down the ice. Rodman fights through his pain and lack of breath and joins Undertaker.

On the other side of the ice, Lovey and Liten block Iggy out of the play. Rapture is behind the play and this leaves Conrad and Milky left skating backwards to defend Rodman and Undertaker.

Right before center ice, Conrad stumbles over his own skates and falls down. Rodman has to jump over him. This leaves just Milky to defend the attack.

Undertaker fakes a shot, draws Milky and Haas towards him, and passes the puck to Rodman.

Haas hits the breaks and falls to one knee.

Rodman catches the pass and lines up his shot

Haas hops up onto his skates and pushes himself with both feet and one hand off the ice into the direction of Rodman's aim.

Rodman fires the puck.

Haas dives through the air towards the puck. He gets the tip of his glove on it, but the puck trickles just beyond Haas' reach, behind him, and into the net.

Rodman raises his flippers and glides past and around the net as the goal lights go off. The slot machine jackpot noise plays over the arena speakers. Rodman jumps up and down triumphantly. He throws his stick into the air and his gloves soon follow. He turns around in time to see not only the guys on the ice, but the guys on the bench coming at him. Undertaker reaches him first and tackles Rodman to the ice with a giant hug. Lovey dives on top of Rodman and Undertaker. Then, Liten, Kane and all five remaining Gamblers, including Safari Chip, roll around the ice in a huge celebratory pile.

Haas and Milky skate dolefully to their bench where some of the Gold Rush players are already trying to exit the ice. Coil stops them, reminding them that they have handshakes yet to give.

Jason stands absolutely stunned at the other end of the ice.

The crowd, especially the Chill and Alston, goes crazy in their seats.

The Gamblers begin to stand up one by one. Kane helps Undertaker up, and they both help Rodman to his feet. They hoist him onto their shoulders. Lovey and Sammie raise Liten onto their shoulders, and Maverick and Goose raise Safari Chip onto theirs. Holding their captain, number one alternate, and their coach, the Gamblers, led by their other alternate captain, Harlan, skate a victory lap around the ice.

The Gold Rush continue to watch the Gamblers celebration in stunned disappointment.

Gamblers and Gold Rush fans alike stick around and give their teams a standing ovation.

Both teams do their customary handshakes. As always, Jason, having learned nothing about sportsmanship, skates off before he can shake hands with Rodman. Coil sees him do it this time, and he reads Jason the riot act as they exit the ice.

Red carpet is laid from the tunnel to center ice. The IAHL president walks down the carpet with the Anderson Cup accompanying directly behind him. The Gamblers, in their championship hats, migrate to and stand around looking at the Cup as it is set upon a table.

The IAHL president holds a microphone. "It is rare in any sport for a team to get off to as bad a start as the Gamblers got off to this season and manage to turn it around. A start as bad as theirs has never been overcome in the IAHL... Until now."

The president has to wait for the crowd to finish going berserk before he can continue.

He tries to speak twice and has to stop. Finally, an ever so slight reduction in noise allows him to sneak back in. "Hockey is not a game won by an individual, and this year's Cup definitely belongs to this entire team. But, the winning started primarily because of two animals. First, I'd like to congratulate Safari Chip on doing whatever it took to turn this team into champions. It is because of your hard work, dedication, and perseverance that I am able to hand to you and your team, with great pleasure, the Anderson Cup."

Safari Chip shakes hands with the president and has the Cup handed to him. He holds the cup over his head and shakes it triumphantly to the delight of the crowd. After a moment that seems to him all too brief, he lowers the trophy to his chest and poses for a picture by one of the many photographers swarming around.

The president raises the microphone again. "I said the winning was primarily due to two animals. Obviously, Safari Chip brought the winning spirit to Las Vegas. And he did that with the discovery and acquisition of a penguin, who albeit was known throughout South Africa as the best player in those parts, was not known until now as probably the best player in all of the world. Rodman T. Penguin has no doubt been the leader, the heart and soul, and the MVP of this team."

Rodman skates to Safari Chip and is handed the Anderson Cup. He wears a smile even bigger than the happy-go-lucky smile he normally wears. He hoists the Cup over his head and takes it for a victory lap around the ice. The crowd cheers and the Gamblers follow close behind. When his lap is over, Rodman hands the Cup to Undertaker.

Undertaker does a smaller victory lap with the Cup in his paws and over his head.

The president wraps up his speech. "Let's hear it one more time for all of the Anderson Cup Champion Las Vegas Gamblers!"

The crowd cheers.

The Cup goes from Undertaker to Kane and round and round until each player has a chance to hoist it and skate a lap. The crowd goes especially nuts for Harlan and Liten, the alternates and two players who overcame more this season than anyone else on the team. Liten is the final Gambler to get a lap with the cup. He's too gimpy to hoist it, so Rodman and Lovey pick him up, set him inside the bowl atop the cup, and push him around the ice.

At the end of Liten's lap, Rodman and Lovey push the cup towards some cameramen at center ice. The rest of the Gamblers follow. Everyone, including Safari Chip, lies in front of, stands next to, sits atop, or piles in where ever they can around the Cup for a championship photo. They all hold up a solitary finger to let the world know they're number one. The picture is taken, and though their magical season ends, the party has just begun. In case of a win, the city has already planned an eight mile parade that will stretch the length of Las Vegas Boulevard from downtown to the end of the Strip.

For the Gamblers, the most exciting part of the win is knowing that this is just the first of many fun and exciting seasons to come.

A special thanks to:

Megan Martino for all your hard work in helping me get this story into the shape it's in and for all the ideas you gave while writing it. I love you Meggy.

Jacob and Paula Blodgett for all the promotion you guys have done and your support of Rodman.

Everyone who loves and supports Rodman T. Penguin.

And of course, Rodman T. Penguin himself.

Look for Hockey Penguin 2 and
Hockey Penguin 3peat available now!

Don't forget to befriend Rodman on Facebook @

www.facebook.com/rodmanthepenguin

There you can find other friends of the Gamblers friends including:

Safari Chip
Liten Mus
Harlan T. Turtle
Morty "Undertaker" Curtains
Keith Kane
Lovey Bara
Sammie Lou
Maverick Limpright
Bruce Goose
Canter L-Rod Jones (of Hockey Penguin 2)
Beary Nelson Riley (of Hockey Penguin 2)
Apple Jack (of Hockey Penguin 2)
Big Chick (of Hockey Penguin 2)
Jason Vyand
Lance Maulbreath

You can also contact the author at:
lvhockeypenguin@yahoo.com or www.facebook.com/thee5hole

Check out hockeypenguin.net to read about the characters, view pictures, and for upcoming Hockey Penguin news and events.

Made in the USA
San Bernardino, CA
02 March 2018